Never Give Up

Read
11-11-21

Never Give Up

PAM HANSON & BARBARA ANDREWS

Guideposts
New York, New York

Never Give Up

ISBN-10: 0-8249-4870-X
ISBN-13: 978-0-8249-4870-2

Published by Guideposts
16 East 34th Street
New York, New York 10016
www.guideposts.org

Distributed by Ideals Publications, a Guideposts company
2630 Elm Hill Pike, Suite 100
Nashville, TN 37214

Guideposts, Ideals and *Tales from Grace Chapel Inn* are registered trademarks of Guideposts.

The characters and events in this book are fictional, and any resemblance to actual persons or events is coincidental.

All Scripture quotations are taken from *The Holy Bible, New International Version*. Copyright © 1973, 1978, 1984 International Bible Society. Used by permission of Zondervan Bible Publishers.

Library of Congress Cataloging-in-Publication Data

Hanson, Pam.
  Never give up / Pam Hanson & Barbara Andrews.
    p. cm. — (Tales from Grace Chapel Inn)
  ISBN-13: 978-0-8249-4870-2
  ISBN-10: 0-8249-4870-X
  I. Andrews, Barbara. II. Title.
  PS3608.A7229N48 2011
  813'.6—dc22

                                        2010030778

Cover by Deborah Chabrian
Design by Marisa Jackson
Typeset by Aptara

Printed and bound in the United States of America
10 9 8 7 6 5 4 3 2 1

Acknowledgments

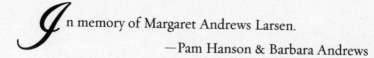In memory of Margaret Andrews Larsen.

—Pam Hanson & Barbara Andrews

GRACE CHAPEL INN

A place where one can be
refreshed and encouraged,
a place of hope and healing,
a place where God is at home.

Never Give Up

Chapter One

*I*t's wonderful to feel a warm breeze on my face."

Alice Howard lowered the window all the way on the passenger side of her sister Louise's old white Cadillac and inhaled the fresh country air.

"You can smell everything budding and blooming," Alice said as she brushed a lock of her bobbed, reddish-brown hair back from her forehead. "I think spring is my favorite season."

"You say that about fall whenever the leaves turn brilliant red and yellow," Louise Smith teased. "And you've been known to say the same thing about winter when the first snow falls in the grove behind the inn."

"You know me too well." Alice laughed softly and closed her eyes to enjoy the wind whipping against her face.

"I should know you after sixty-two years," her sister said. "I can remember when our parents brought you home from the hospital as a newborn."

"You were only a baby yourself!" Alice said, feigning disbelief.

"I was three years old, and your arrival made a big impression on me. I was worried because you were practically bald."

"You didn't have that worry with Jane. When I first saw her as a baby, her hair was long and dark and full," Alice said.

"I don't think you ever played with dolls after Jane was born," Louise mused. "You were much more interested in taking care of a real baby. No one was surprised when you decided to become a nurse."

"I was twelve years old when she was born," Alice reminded her sister. "It was time to pack away my dolls. I envied you, you know. I wanted to be the babysitter when Father needed one, but you were always the one he picked."

Louise smiled, remembering how badly Alice wished she were the oldest sister when they were young.

"You were the one Jane followed like a little puppy," Louise pointed out. "I'm only sorry that she has no memories of Mother. She made life such fun, and our sister missed out on that."

"I remember the wonderful costumes she made for us," Alice reminisced. "When I needed one for an autumn pageant at school, she sewed real leaves on a long tan dress. It was as beautiful as it was original."

Louise slowed the car to a crawl when she came up behind a gravel truck with bits of the load escaping where the tarp had worked loose. As soon as oncoming traffic allowed, she passed the slower vehicle, avoiding the shower of little stones that could chip her windshield.

"I'm always getting stuck behind slow trucks these days," Alice said. "I have to allow extra time to get to the hospital, especially when I start work at three in the afternoon. I wish there was a four-lane highway between Potterston and Acorn Hill."

"If there were, Potterston would probably expand and swallow up our little town," Louise said in her usual practical way.

"You're probably right. Anyway, I'm glad you came with me to the hospital today. I do get tired of driving back and forth to Potterston. It's so relaxing to be a passenger instead of the driver, especially at dusk when it's hard to see. You're such a good driver that I can just relax and enjoy the scenery for a change."

"Thank you for your vote of confidence. I've always enjoyed driving."

"I remember how you breezed through your driving test. You made it seem easy, but when my turn came, I was scared silly."

"You didn't let a little nervousness stop you from getting your license," Louise pointed out.

"Well, anyway, thank you for coming with me to visit Mary. I absolutely adore her, and I was afraid I wouldn't get to see her while she was still in the hospital. I'm not scheduled to work until the weekend. She may be released tomorrow or Friday at the latest, so I would have missed her."

"She talked a mile a minute. I haven't laughed so hard in ages, not what I expected from a hospital visit. It's hard to believe she's ninety-two," Louise said. "I really enjoyed meeting her."

"I've known her for quite a few years, always as a patient. She's had more than her share of health scares, but she's always rallied and gone home to her own little house in Potterston. That's exactly what she's planning to do this time."

"I loved her story about scolding a yardman because he didn't pick up all the black walnuts that fell on her property from her neighbor's tree."

"She's certainly feisty. How many women her age would decide that she was the only one who would do the job correctly? She must have filled two trash cans with rotting nuts from last year," Alice said.

"I once watched Jane pound some open to extract the nutmeats for her black walnut cake," Louise said. "By comparison, they make coconuts look as easy to open as eggshells."

"Only a gourmet chef like our Jane would go to that much trouble for black walnuts," Alice said with a soft laugh, putting the window halfway up and running her fingers through windblown hair.

A pickup truck streaked past them and cut back in front of Louise's car, forcing her to apply the brakes.

"Really!" Louise said. "Drivers like that take the pleasure out of driving. Fortunately, most of the drivers who use this road are courteous and cautious, though this is my least favorite time to be on the highway. It's not quite light and not completely dark. Dusk can play tricks on your eyes."

"I agree," her sister said. "I would rather drive home late at night after my evening shift when it's completely dark. There's almost no traffic then. The countryside seems so tranquil after I've had a busy day at the hospital."

They drove in companionable silence for several minutes, each lost in her own thoughts. They lived together and were partners with their sister Jane in running Grace Chapel Inn, a bed-and-breakfast in the big Victorian house their minister father had left to them. Because they were so close, they never felt a need to fill every minute together with conversation.

"Look out!" Alice cried out, straining forward in her seat belt and unconsciously bracing herself against the dashboard.

Louise had started to slow the car an instant before her sister's warning. She eased it onto the shoulder of the road, her shoulders and arms rigid with tension as she came to a stop.

"Oh dear, oh dear," Alice murmured as she fumbled to release the seat belt and open the door.

"I've never come so close to hitting a deer," Louise said breathlessly. "Oh, I would have felt terrible."

"It's amazing you didn't!" Alice stepped outside the car and squinted to see the small creature weaving slowly beside the road twenty or so yards ahead of them. "But I'm afraid another car will come and not see it. Maybe I can scare it back to the woods."

"Why, it's only a fawn," Louise said, getting out on the driver's side.

Both sisters hurried toward the delicate little creature. They waved their arms and made shooing noises, but the baby deer remained perilously close to the blacktop.

"The mother must be somewhere nearby," Alice said.

"We'd better back off. Maybe we're scaring the doe away from her fawn." Louise stopped waving and looked in all directions.

"I'm afraid it will run onto the road and get hit." Alice checked the highway and was grateful that no headlights were in sight.

She walked farther down the roadway, putting herself between the fawn and danger. Louise made cooing sounds and gestured toward the woods, but the fawn seemed rooted to its spot.

Alice slowly took a few steps closer.

"Please, baby, get away from the road," she begged. "It's almost dark. Cars won't be able to see you."

"I'm surprised it's let us get this close." Louise sounded as worried as Alice felt.

After several anxious moments, the fawn took a few unsteady steps toward the woods. Alice breathed a sigh of relief, but the tiny deer didn't head for the shelter of the trees. Instead it seemed stunned and confused, unsure where to find safety.

"The mother won't come while we're so close," Louise said. "Come back to the car. We've probably done all we can."

"We can't just abandon it," Alice said, but she followed her sister back to the car, quietly closing the door after she slipped inside. "Let's just watch for a while. I won't feel right leaving until I'm sure the mother comes for her baby."

Louise switched the headlights of her car to parking lights, making it more difficult to see what the fawn was doing.

"It will be fully dark soon," Alice pointed out needlessly. "Where *is* that mother?"

"Look. The fawn is lying down."

"Maybe making itself smaller to blend in with the surroundings," Alice speculated. "I've read that fawns do that to camouflage themselves. Sometimes a doe has to go farther than the fawn can follow in order to eat enough to make rich milk."

"That shouldn't be the case now. There's fresh green foliage everywhere."

"Let's wait a little longer. A fawn is such a helpless little creature," Alice said.

A van passed, and the sisters exchanged a look. If they hadn't herded the fawn back from the road, it might have been hit.

"I feel responsible for it," Alice said, expressing what they both felt.

The last streaks of orange disappeared beyond the horizon, and the first star twinkled in the velvet blue of the sky. The fawn stayed as still as a statue, patiently waiting for a mother that didn't come.

"I don't know what to do," Alice said. "If we take it with us, the mother will never find her baby."

"But if something has happened to the mother, does the fawn have a chance of surviving on its own?"

"We can't sit here all night," Alice lamented. "Jane is probably worried about us already."

"We can't stay, and we can't leave." Louise said. "We need help."

"Someone who knows more about deer than we do," Alice agreed. "I'm sure Mark could tell us what to do."

"Good idea. Maybe we can flag down someone with a cell phone, and you can call him."

Alice felt hopeful as Louise stepped out of the car to wait for a passing motorist to stop. Mark was the chief veterinarian for the Philadelphia Zoo and a longtime friend of Alice. He'd been her college beau, and she knew he would give them the best possible advice.

They didn't have long to wait. By happy chance, a car pulled in behind them within minutes. Alice stepped out of the Cadillac and went to Louise's side just as a familiar voice greeted them.

"Louise. And Alice. Are you having car trouble? I'll be happy to give you a lift into town." Viola Reed's imposing figure approached them, her long signature scarf swaying behind her.

"No, not car trouble," Louise said, greeting the owner of Acorn Hill's Nine Lives Bookstore.

She'd never flagged down a car before this, so it was a relief to have a friend stop.

"Viola, are we glad to see you. Look over there," Alice said.

Their friend peered ahead, but her bifocals weren't up to letting her see the little deer pressed close to the ground.

"We spotted a fawn when it was in danger of wandering onto the road," Alice explained. "We've been waiting for the mother to come for it, but so far she hasn't showed up. We don't know whether we should take it with us or leave it."

"Afraid that's not my area of expertise," Viola said as the wind ruffled her short steel-gray hair and threatened to snatch away her bright green-and-gold silk scarf.

"Is there any chance you have a cell phone we could use?" Louise asked. "Alice's friend Mark Graves will know what we should do."

"I surely do," Viola said. "Let me fetch it from the car."

"Do you know Mark's number?" Louise asked her sister while they waited for Viola to sort through the papers and bags on the front seat and return with the cell phone.

"I'm so rattled, I probably can't remember my own phone number," Alice admitted. "But you know I always carry a little address book in my purse."

"I'd forgotten," Louise admitted. "I must be rattled too. I keep thinking how easily I could have hit the fawn. If it had decided to bound across the road, I wouldn't have been able to stop in time."

"I'm confident you would have managed to miss it," Alice reassured her. "You have good reflexes, and you're always alert. Maybe it comes with being a musician. You don't miss a note, driving or playing the piano."

"And you always know the right thing to say." Louise gave her sister a little hug of thanks as Viola walked toward them.

"Let's all sit in the car, then I can use the dome light to find Mark's number," Alice suggested.

Louise got behind the wheel again and started the engine so the lights wouldn't drain the battery. She peered through the windshield, still hoping the mother would come for her baby. Alice got into the backseat with Viola and dug into her tan shoulder-strap bag. The little notebook of addresses and phone numbers had made its way to the very bottom, and it took her a minute to find it.

"I hope we're not keeping you from something," she said apologetically to Viola.

"Oh no, I'm just heading home from dinner in Potterston. A bunch of booksellers in the county get together once a month and talk shop. It's always nice to hear which books are selling well in other stores and how they're solving business problems. Of course, when you get book-lovers together, there's no end of things to talk about."

"It sounds like fun," Alice said absentmindedly, finally locating her address book.

She found Mark's office and home phone numbers. Viola explained how to use the cell phone, and Alice punched in his home number. It seemed odd to be using such a tiny instrument, but in a moment she heard ringing on his end. His answering machine picked up, not Mark, much to her disappointment.

"Mark, it's Alice. Louise and I have found a fawn along the road, and the mother hasn't come to claim it. We're not sure what to do."

She waited a minute, hoping he was there and would pick up. When that didn't happen, she broke the connection.

"He could be working late. I'll try his office number too."

Again she got a recorded message.

"Now I really don't know what we should do," Alice said dejectedly. "We can't stay here much longer, but I have a bad feeling about leaving the fawn alone."

"They're so helpless when they're little, aren't they?" Viola took the cell phone back from Alice but made no move to leave. "There must be someone else you can call. Who in the area knows a lot about animals?"

"Of course!" Louise said. "Jack O'Hara. We should have thought of him first."

"He loves animals," Viola agreed. "I've ordered lots of wildlife books for him. I've always thought it was nice that he could make a living as an animal control officer. He has a real gift for getting along with furry and feathered creatures."

"Best of all, he works out of Potterston. He must know this road like the back of his hand," Alice said. "But I don't think I have his number in my book."

"No problem," Viola said. "I always carry last year's phone book in my car in case I have trouble on the road or something. Just let me go look."

While Viola searched in the cluttered trunk of her car for the elusive phone directory, Alice stepped along the edge of the highway, trying to get a glimpse of the fawn. A passing car briefly illuminated the spot where it had settled. The little creature was still there, head upright, waiting for its mother. All Alice's instincts wanted to cradle the frightened baby deer in her arms, but she was sure that was exactly the wrong thing to do. It was a wild animal, not used to humans. If she even tried to get close, it might bolt onto the highway. Alice couldn't shake the feeling that something bad had happened to the mother.

When she got back to the car, Louise had already talked to Jack.

"He's coming to take a look himself," she said with relief. "He said we were absolutely right to watch but not try to pick it up. The mother would probably still take it back if we had touched it, but there's a real danger of frightening a young fawn into a state of shock."

Alice rejoined Viola on the backseat.

"I'm so grateful that you were passing just when we needed you," she said.

"So am I. Now I'm as worried about the fawn as you are. Fortunately, Jack will be here in no time at all."

Louise fell into an anxious silence while Alice tried to keep up a conversation with Viola. The bookstore owner knew about Alice's love of mysteries, and Alice was a frequent browser in Nine Lives Bookstore, which Viola ran with a style all her own. The bookseller had very strong ideas about literature. She loved classics and had little use for most contemporary fiction, but she did keep a stock of mysteries for good customers like Alice.

"How are things at the inn?" Viola asked.

"Oh, just fine," Alice said. We'll probably have all four guest rooms filled most of the summer. Of course, things are a little slow now, but we're looking forward to having two newcomers this week, two women from Kalamazoo."

"Kal-a-ma-zoo," Viola said sounding out the name. "I've always liked the sound of it, but I've never met anyone who lived there."

"Well, they'll be vacationing here for almost two weeks," Alice said, "so maybe you'll get a chance to meet them. I don't know what their plans are, but I'll certainly recommend Nine Lives Bookstore as a place to visit in Acorn Hill if they ask."

"Nice of you," Viola said absentmindedly.

"I hope nothing happens to the fawn before Jack gets here," Alice said, voicing everyone's concern.

"Car pulling over," Louise called out after what seemed like an hour but was less then fifteen minutes.

The three of them got out of the car and waited anxiously as a vehicle parked on the other side of the road. Much to their relief, the familiar figure of Jack O'Hara crossed the highway and walked toward them. Alice had never been so glad to see the redheaded former marine.

"I've got bad news," he said solemnly after a brief greeting.

He hesitated, pulling on one end of his luxuriant handlebar mustache.

"About the doe?" Alice asked.

"Yeah, I found her alongside the road about a half mile back. She was hit by something big and heavy by the looks of it, most likely a truck. I'm afraid what you have is an orphan fawn."

"Oh, poor thing!" Louise said. "I was hoping the mother would come to claim it."

"What about the father?" Viola asked.

"Mother deer raise the babies," Jack said. "Your little fawn is on its own, and I wouldn't get too hopeful about its chances of survival."

"Then we have to do something," Alice said decisively.

"It's not as easy as you might think," Jack said in a kind voice. "It's a wild creature. Contact with humans could be fatal. You can't hold it or pet it like you would a puppy or a kitty. And there are serious feeding concerns. Most human and pet food will kill it. Then if you do manage to save it, it could get downright dangerous to have around, especially if it's a male."

"What will happen to it if we leave it here?" Louise asked.

Jack shook his head and looked down at the scruffy running shoes he was wearing off duty.

"I hate to say it, because I love dogs, but a deer's worst enemies, aside from human hunters, are canines. Out here in the country, there are sure to be farmers' dogs that get loose from time to time. Sometimes they even form packs. They'll take down a helpless fawn just because it's in their nature to hunt."

"Oh, that's awful," Viola moaned.

"If dogs don't get the fawn, what can it eat in the wild?" Louise asked.

"Without its mother's milk, it will starve. Whitetails like we have here in Pennsylvania are usually born in May, so the little orphan can't be very old even if it came early."

"Then we have to do what we can," Alice said.

"Just so you know, there's only a small chance of raising it successfully and returning it to the wild," Jack said, obviously unhappy at being the bearer of bad news.

"The first thing is to get it home," Louise said. "Fortunately we have the gardening shed to house it temporarily."

"Even that won't be as easy as it sounds," Jack said.

Alice knew that Jack was usually a positive person, good-natured and smiling. If he warned against the difficulties, the task had to be exceptionally hard. Still, she couldn't leave the fawn—she already thought of it as "her" fawn—to starve or be hunted.

"I still have a blanket in the trunk of the car that I keep for winter emergencies," Louise said. "Will that help?"

"More than anything I can offer," Jack said glumly. "My dog Roscoe has been all over my car. It will be traumatic enough for the fawn to deal with human scents. I can't subject her to canine scents too."

"So tell us what to do," Viola said with concern. "Can we use the blanket to carry the fawn?"

"Good suggestion," Jack said. "We'll spread it out, and one of you will have to lift it carefully onto the middle of the blanket. Roscoe was napping on my lap, so I probably smell as doggy as he does."

Alice was a little cheered by the thought of the chubby black terrier curled up for a nap, but Jack had certainly impressed upon her the seriousness of the present situation. Still, a fawn was one of God's creatures, and Alice knew she had to do her best for it.

Dear God, Please guide me. Don't let my actions harm an innocent creature, she silently prayed.

The four of them walked down the road with Jack's flashlight lighting the way. The fawn was just as they'd last seen it, body flattened to the ground as it instinctively tried to hide itself. Alice's eyes teared at the sight of the patient little creature.

At Jack's direction, the three women spread the thick red plaid blanket near the fawn as it listlessly watched. Alice volunteered to lift the fawn. She wasn't sure how to manage it, fearing especially that it would resist. Although it wasn't large or especially heavy for a nurse used to moving human patients, there were four gangly legs to concern her. Surprisingly, the fawn's defensive tactic was to hold its legs tight against its body as she tried to pick it up.

Much to the collective relief of all four of them, Alice managed to move the fawn and gently set it down in the center of the outspread blanket.

"Now we can all take a corner," Jack directed. "Get a good grip, and tell me when you're ready to lift."

Alice wrapped her corner of the blanket around her hand as best she could so there was no possibility of letting it slip away. The others did the same, then they slowly and carefully lifted. The fawn was light, and sharing the burden among four adults made it easy. In the process, though, Jack had to extinguish his flashlight. Alice was in the rear with Louise while Jack and Viola led the way to the car in the dark.

Viola was wearing high heels and a long skirt that nearly brushed the ground. Alice held her breath, hoping their friend wouldn't stumble and become another casualty. She couldn't help noticing that Jack was edging along backward, keeping his hand under the weight of the fawn in the center of the blanket and obviously ready for any misstep on the part of anyone else. She was thankful that they had been able to call on him.

The best way to transport the fawn seemed to be on the backseat of Louise's car. Although Jack warned that the scent of humans was likely to upset the fawn, he had to agree that Alice should ride in back to prevent the baby deer from panicking.

"Wait here a minute," Jack said.

He jogged to his car and returned with an unopened bottle of water.

"I don't know how long it's been without water," he said, uncapping the water and moistening a big white handkerchief.

He squeezed a few drops into the fawn's mouth, but the animal was unresponsive as far as Alice could see. After a couple of tries, Jack poured water on the hanky and squeezed the excess out over the ground. Then he gently spread it over the fawn's eyes and bunched up the blanket to make a cocoon of sorts.

"I'll meet you at the inn to help you unload," he said, running the back of his hand across his forehead in a gesture of concern. "Fortunately you're pretty close to home."

Viola went back to her car and declared that she wouldn't be able to sleep that night unless she saw the fawn safely bedded down. Led by Louise, they made a small procession toward Acorn Hill.

Alice had never been more grateful for Louise's careful handling of the big old Cadillac. The ride was as smooth as it could be, and she finally breathed a sigh of relief when they parked in front of Grace Chapel Inn.

"You've made it this far, baby," Alice whispered to the fawn. "With God's help and good friends, you're going to be all right."

Chapter Two

Alice slid out of the back of the car and was surprised to find herself trembling. It wasn't because a chill wind had swept away the warmth of the May day. In fact, the evening was balmy. She hugged her arms against herself, trying in vain to still the trembling so no one would notice her nervousness.

This was so unlike her. The responsibility she had undertaken left her unsettled, all the more surprising because she was accustomed to handling emergencies at the hospital. This was totally different, however. She'd taken on the care of a wild creature in a situation where she might do more harm than good.

Their little caravan of cars was lined up in front of Grace Chapel Inn, the closest they could get to the gardening shed that would serve as a temporary refuge for the fawn. Alice tried to imagine the scene as the fawn was seeing it. The poor thing had to be terrified of the huge alien beings clustered around the strange contraption that had brought it to this place.

Alice's brain buzzed with unanswered questions. How well could a fawn see at night or any other time for that matter? It was too young to process the nearness of so many strange creatures. How was it faring with the noise of their presence? Even though all of them were speaking in whispers, the deer's keen hearing probably magnified their words into odd blasts of sound. And the smells! How could a wild creature possibly deal with all the scents of a human gathering?

The fawn was deathly still in the refuge they had made of the blanket. Under the dome light of the car, Alice could see white spots on its reddish-brown back, part of the camouflage that protected very young whitetails. Its large, dark eyes looked fearful, and a soft bleating sound rose up from deep in its chest, a call to a mother that would never come.

Even Jack, take-charge guy that he was, seemed a little hesitant about what to do next. Viola had gotten out of her car and was staring at the fawn with the same look of awe that Alice knew must be etched on her own face.

"Are we going to carry it on the blanket again?" Viola asked.

"Maybe I should take a look inside that shed before we move it," Jack said. "Make sure there aren't any obvious hazards. Poor little thing is scared enough without a rake or something falling on it."

"That's a good idea," Louise said. "I'll show you the way."

The two of them went up the walk and around the side of the long front porch, disappearing into a garden illuminated only by light spilling out of the kitchen window.

Jane must have heard sounds outside the inn, because the porch light went on and the front door opened.

"What's going on?" she called as she started toward them.

"We have a surprise guest," Alice said softly as soon as her sister was close enough to hear. "Viola and Jack O'Hara helped us put it in the car."

"Where on earth did you find it?" Jane asked when she caught a glimpse of the fawn huddled on the backseat.

"We saw it alone by the side of the road on our way home. We tried to shoo it into the woods so it wouldn't get hit by a car, but all it did was hunker down."

"The mother will miss it," Jane said. "Why bring it here?"

"We called Jack to ask him for help, and on his drive out to us, he saw the doe dead beside the road. There's no way a fawn this young can survive on its own."

"Oh my!" Jane bent and studied their unusual passenger. "Poor thing. What are you going to do with it?"

"Put it in the shed for now. I called Mark to ask his advice, but he wasn't home. I'm hoping he'll call back tonight."

"It's not quite like taking in a stray cat, is it?" Jane asked thoughtfully. "I wonder what it will eat. It was probably dependent on its mother's milk."

"I hope Mark can tell us that."

"It's awfully quiet, not trying to escape or anything." Jane sounded worried.

"We think it's too young to have developed many survival skills. All it knows how to do is make itself small and try to stay camouflaged."

"It will need water," Jane said, sounding relieved to think of something she could provide. "I'll get a clean bowl and pour in some bottled water."

"Good idea," Alice said. "And turn on the light by the side door so we can see to carry it to the shed."

"Do you need me to help?"

"The four of us can manage," Viola said, confirming that she too felt responsible for the fawn.

"Oh, sorry if I seemed to ignore you, Viola," Jane said with an embarrassed smile. "I was so stunned to see a deer riding in Louise's car that I didn't focus on anything else."

"I know exactly what you mean," Viola assured her.

"Louise and Jack are checking out the shed for hazards," Alice said. "It's the only place I could think to put it."

"I suppose it will do temporarily." Jane sounded doubtful. "Maybe I'd better remind Louise to open the little window over the workbench. The ventilation still won't be great, but it will help."

Alice murmured encouragement, and Jane hurried off to help check out the shed.

"The handkerchief fell off its eyes," Viola said pointing to the bit of rumpled white cloth that lay in the fold of the blanket.

Alice retrieved the hanky but didn't know whether to place it over the fawn's eyes again. There were so many things she didn't know about taking care of a fawn.

"I can't think of any book at the store that would tell us what to do," Viola mused. "We don't even know whether we're dealing with a doe or a buck."

"I guess we'd better hope it's female," Alice said. "It might stay more docile."

She hadn't thought about gender yet, but Jack had suggested that a young buck could be difficult to handle when it grew bigger. How fast did a deer mature? That was something else she didn't know. She'd always been enchanted to glimpse deer in the wild. They were such stately, graceful creatures. As a motorist, she was wary of their crossing the highway, but as a person who loved nature, she always reflected on the wonder of God's creation when she saw one.

Viola fell silent, and Alice found herself without anything to say. It seemed to be taking forever for the others to check out the shed. Her biggest worry was that the fawn would try to escape from the confines of the car. It could injure itself attempting to get away. For now, though, the poor thing seemed frozen in place, too terrified to take any action.

Something brushed against Alice's ankle, and she started in surprise.

"Wendell!"

The gray-and-black striped tabby must have followed Jane when she left the inn. Ordinarily Alice would have scooped him up for a little cuddle, something she enjoyed as much as the cat did. This evening she was leery of introducing any more alien scents into the fawn's world.

"Oh, it's your kitty," Viola said, not hesitating to stoop and stroke his head. "Now if we'd found a stray cat, I would know what to do."

Alice smiled. Viola was a cat lover to the core, sharing her home with a host of felines named after her favorite literary characters.

"I don't know how our visitor will react to a cat," Alice said with a worried frown.

"Do you want me to put him back in the house?" Viola asked, already in the process of picking him up.

"That's a good idea, thank you."

Viola took Wendell toward the porch, while Alice studied the fawn. Lifting it out of the car was going to be tricky. What if the little creature panicked and tried to resist them? It would be awful if the infant deer injured itself, adding to the trauma it was already experiencing. They needed to put it in a safe place to rest and gain strength. Why was it taking her sisters and Jack so long to check out the shed? It shouldn't require more than a minute or two to remove the lawn mower and snow blower and clear out any garden equipment that might prove dangerous.

Alice's instinct was to pet the fawn, but she was afraid it wouldn't be soothed by stroking. She felt so helpless not being able to offer any form of comfort. She kept reminding herself that this was a wild animal, no matter how adorable it seemed.

Viola returned just as the others came around the porch and headed toward the car.

"I think it will be all right as a temporary shelter," Louise pronounced. "Jack cleared out the lawn mower, rakes and such. Jane broke off some small, leafy branches to make a bed on the floor."

"Not as good as straw," Jane said, "but I thought some new growth from the bushes behind the house would give the shed a more natural smell."

"That's a good idea," Alice said, although she wasn't sure that Jane's efforts would comfort the fawn. "It may be a problem lifting it out of the car. I think one person should do it."

"I'll take care of that," Jack offered.

"Thank you, but I think I should do it," Alice said with more confidence than she felt. "I'm used to moving patients at the hospital. The fawn weighs a lot less than some of the children I lift every day."

"I don't want you to hurt yourself," Louise said protectively. "If your patients kick, at least they don't have hooves."

"I'm sure Alice knows what she's doing," Jane said. "Maybe we should all stand back and give her space."

"If you're sure," Jack said.

Alice silently prayed that she wouldn't injure the fawn, then reached into the car and scooped it up, blanket and all. The smell of the deer was strong in her nostrils, and she could feel as well as hear the creature's alarmed bleating as she hugged it against her.

"Do you want help now?" Viola asked, sounding uncharacteristically anxious.

"No, I'm afraid that putting it down so all of us can carry it on the blanket will be more traumatic than going straight to the shed."

Jack held his flashlight and led the way, and the others followed Alice and the fawn. Alice didn't think about how heavy her burden was. She had a strange sense of unreality, a feeling that she'd stepped into a world where she might not belong. She fervently hoped that their good intentions wouldn't be disastrous for one of God's innocent creatures.

"I'll get the door," Jack said, stepping ahead but keeping his flashlight trained on the ground to help Alice with her footing.

The small light over the side door of the house spilled weakly onto the lawn in front of the shed. Alice went into the small structure by herself and gently laid the fawn on the carpet of branches that Jane had spread out, letting the blanket fall free so she could remove it.

"I think it will be warm enough," she said, grateful for the mild spring evening.

She stooped and moved the water dish closer to the branches, reluctant to leave the fawn alone.

"I think that's all we can do for now," Jack said in a kind voice.

"Maybe I should sit with it for a while." The nurse in Alice wouldn't let her abandon any creature that needed her.

"If Mark phones back, you'll want to be in the house to take his call," Louise said.

"There's nothing you can do now," Jack said, giving her encouragement to leave the fawn by itself.

"You're right, of course," Alice agreed, but she lingered a few more moments while the others backed away from the shed.

"I knew Louise and Alice might be late, so I have dinner waiting for them," Jane said to Viola and Jack. "There's plenty for all. I hope you'll both join us."

"Oh dear, I've already had dinner," Viola said regretfully.

"You're welcome to stay for coffee and dessert," Jane said.

"Thank you, Jane. I'd love to, but I think I'd better get home and check on my cats. Tess, my little stray from the school yard, is in a family way. I'll call tomorrow and see how the fawn is doing. If there's anything I can do, please let me know. I'll see if I can locate a book on how to raise a fawn. Maybe I can print out some information from the Internet too."

"That would be wonderful. You saved the day when you stopped with your cell phone," Alice said gratefully. "Thank you so much for your help."

"We did have a little adventure, didn't we?" Viola said. "I just hope the poor thing will be all right."

"Jack, you'll stay, won't you?" Jane asked as Viola walked toward her car.

"My pleasure. I was just about to put one of those king-size TV dinners in the microwave when I got the call. It's Alison's eat-and-deal night. That's what I call my wife's bridge club. You know how she likes to play."

"You're welcome to have your boys come over," Jane said. "I think I can stretch dinner to take care of three more hearty appetites."

"Their mother left them a Crock-Pot of chili. The rascals polished off the whole thing before I got home from work," he said, obviously proud of his sons' good appetites. "So I'm an unfed bachelor at the moment. To tell the truth, I'd rescue a grizzly for one of your meals, Jane."

"I hope you won't be disappointed," Jane said with a warm smile.

Alice stayed behind as her sisters and Jack went through the side door to the kitchen. Reluctantly she closed the shed door and secured the lock that held it shut. All her instincts made her yearn to stay with the fawn, but she had to listen to reason. She hoped that Mark would call as soon as he got home and give her the benefit of his experience as a vet. Until then, she could only pray that the poor little fawn would be all right.

Chapter Three

*L*ouise was a little concerned because Alice stayed outside instead of following them to the kitchen. She knew that her sister felt things deeply and that she was worried about the fawn. They all were, but Alice was sure to think that she was primarily responsible for its welfare.

Jack made himself at home in the big, comfy kitchen. People tended to do that, Louise knew, but it wasn't just the cheerful black-and-white checkerboard floor, rusty-red cupboards and maple butcher-block countertops that made the room so welcoming. Jane had made it her domain in more than the physical sense. She was always happy when she was busy with her pots and pans, and her warmth radiated throughout the room. She loved cooking, putting her professional chef's skills to work daily by preparing the luscious breakfasts that helped attract visitors to their bed-and-breakfast. To her, cooking was an art, and she practiced it daily in every meal the family enjoyed.

Better still, Jane loved company, and a last-minute guest never fazed her in the least. Jack was an especially appreciative diner, and he didn't hesitate to check the oven of the big gas stove to see what was filling the room with an appetizing aroma.

"Chicken tetrazzini," Jane said with a smile, her dark ponytail dancing as she added a plate for Jack to the kitchen table where the sisters had their meals.

In faded jeans and a bright yellow T-shirt with a flower motif she'd painted herself, Jane didn't look like a typical major-league chef, but her meals were any restaurant's equal. She had the gift of making food look as appetizing as it tasted, something Louise, whose skills didn't lie in that direction, greatly appreciated.

Far from resenting Jack's look into her oven, Jane was more than happy to talk about her latest creation.

"I had homemade mushroom soup left over from lunch yesterday, and I'm using it for this recipe. And, of course, I grate my own cheese. The grated cheese they sell in bags loses too much flavor."

"Is that dill I smell?" Jack asked with an appreciative sniff.

Louise had to smile at his enthusiasm. Jack was an ex-marine who maintained his military bearing years after retiring from the corps. He wore his bright-red hair in a crew cut, kept his handlebar mustache neatly trimmed and wore his uniform with an air of command. Even in the casual khaki slacks, green-and-navy striped soccer shirt, and running shoes that he wore this evening, he gave the impression that he was in control. He was also a man with an optimistic outlook on life. He didn't suffer fools gladly, but he had a warm side that had made him a friend of the Howard sisters.

Jack adored his family and devoted much of his free time to the sports and activities of his three sons. He also loved animals, approaching his job as an animal control officer for the county with genuine concern for wild and domestic creatures. In his spare time he played an active part in the community and sang in the choir at Grace Chapel, the church where the sisters' late father, Daniel Howard, had served as minister for many years.

"You have a good nose," Jane said. "That's warm dill bread to go with the tetrazzini. Here, you can put it on the table."

She handed him a basket lined with a pale-yellow linen cloth that was draped over the bread to keep it warm.

"Guess I'm lucky the boys polished off Alison's chili," he said with a chuckle.

It was well known that his wife was a lovely person but not the best of cooks. She was famous for buying angel food cakes at the grocery store and covering them with canned frosting for church potlucks.

"We're fortunate that you answered our distress call," Louise said. "We didn't have a clue what to do about the fawn."

"Any time I can help the Howard sisters, it's my privilege," Jack said in a courtly tone. "And this time it was for a particularly good cause. I have no doubt that the fawn wouldn't have survived if we'd left it. That's the only justification for removing a wild animal from its habitat. We'll just have to hope it's strong enough to make it."

Both sisters murmured agreement.

Jane was nearly ready to serve dinner, and Louise was ready to find their sister and convince her to join them, when Alice came into the kitchen.

Alice smiled as she commented on the delicious smell emanating from the heavy ironstone casserole dish that Jane had placed on the table, but her mind seemed somewhere else, no doubt back in the shed with the fawn.

Jane put a bowl of fresh spinach salad and a cruet of her special tomato vinaigrette dressing on the table and invited everyone to sit down.

Louise asked Jack to lead them in a blessing, and he quickly assented.

"Lord, thank You for the gifts we are about to receive and for the friendship that brought us to together," he said in his rich baritone voice. "Bless the fawn You have given into our care. Help us to do it no harm. In Christ's name we pray. Amen."

"Now if everyone will give me a plate, I'll serve," Jane said. "The dish is too hot to pass."

"Just a small serving for me, please," Alice said.

Louise knew this was a sure sign that her sister was upset. The tetrazzini with chicken and spaghetti noodles in Jane's luscious cheese-and-mushroom sauce was one of Alice's favorite dishes.

"We need to find a place where the fawn can be outside until it's strong enough to be released," Alice said, letting her food sit untouched on her plate.

"Maybe a farm," Jane suggested.

"That's something I can look into," Jack said. "This is wonderful, Jane. Best meal I've had since Alison and I went to the Knife and Fork in Potterston for our anniversary. In fact, this is better. Their chef is a little heavy-handed with the sage in his stuffed pork chops."

"Thank you," Jane said, her blue eyes sparkling at the compliment. "I love cooking for people who appreciate my efforts."

With her cheeks still flushed pink from the heat of the oven, Jane looked younger than her fifty years and pretty in a slightly mischievous way. Sometimes Louise felt more motherly than sisterly toward her youngest sibling, not surprising since she'd partly filled the role of the mother Jane had never known. But this evening it was Alice who concerned her. They had to face the fact that the fawn might not survive without its mother, and it was going to be especially hard on Alice if they lost it.

"I'm still hoping Mark will call this evening," Alice said as she absentmindedly twirled a bit of pasta around her fork. "He could be out of town, of course. He travels quite a bit giving lectures for the zoo."

"Good idea to check with a vet," Jack agreed, helping himself to another slice of dill bread from the basket.

"We could call Dr. Ferris in Potterston," Jane suggested. "He seems very helpful and knowledgeable when I take Wendell for his shots and such."

"I've heard he's very good with pets," Alice said, "but we don't know if he's had any experience with wild animals. I'll try again to reach Mark if we don't hear from him soon."

"I hope you'll like our buttermilk sherbet," Jane said, sensing Alice's unease and trying to change the subject for the moment. "You may know, Jack, that Louise loves anything with buttermilk. It's her favorite beverage, and Louie's luscious sherbet is one of her favorite desserts."

"It's actually a delicious pineapple treat," Louise said, not showing a reaction to Jane's use of her childhood nickname. "You don't have to be a fan of buttermilk to enjoy it, and even I can mix it up in a jiffy."

Jack volunteered to help clear away the plates when everyone had finished. Jane took away her sister's half-full plate without comment, knowing that Alice didn't have much appetite when her concerns left her unsettled. Louise was concerned about the fawn, too, and it bothered her that there was nothing she could do for it at the moment. Jane served the frozen dessert in glass sherbet dishes and set out a plate of tiny vanilla cookies sparkling with a very light coating of sugar. Jack couldn't seem to compliment her cooking enough, and to the delight of Louise as well as Jane, he singled out the buttermilk sherbet for special praise.

"I'm afraid I have to eat and run," Jack said after a second helping of the sherbet, which Louise had dished up for him. "Have to check on the homework situation. If I don't ride herd on those rascals of mine, they'll conveniently forget to do it."

"Thank you again, Jack. I don't know what we would have done without you," Alice said.

"Glad to help. You keep me posted, and I'll see what I can do about finding a temporary place for the fawn. Good night, ladies."

"I wonder if I should check on it before I go to bed?" Alice asked.

"Maybe it's best to let it get used to the shed before we disturb it again," Louise suggested tactfully.

"We tried to remove everything that could possibly harm it," Jack said. "It's probably as safe as it can be."

"Oh, by the way, Louise," Jane said, "we've been so distracted by the fawn that I forgot to give you a message. In fact, several messages from the same person. A woman named Lara Zale wants you to go to her house for tea tomorrow afternoon."

"I don't think I know that name," Alice said as she rinsed dishes before putting them in the dishwasher.

"She's the mother of my new pupil," Louise said. "Her daughter Diana is promising to be one of my better students. She had quite a few years of piano before they moved to Acorn Hill. I'm excited to be working with her. Not only does she have talent, she has a very good attitude. I've only given her half a dozen lessons, but it's obvious that she dedicates a lot of time to practicing. She's more than meeting my expectations."

"Mrs. Zale said she would check with you in the morning to see if four o'clock is a convenient time," Jane said, reading a note she'd left near the kitchen phone.

"I wonder why she wants to see me. Parents who want to stop lessons usually do so by phone. Or they tell me when they pick up their child. I would really hate to lose Diana after such a short time."

"Maybe she just wants to give you more information about her daughter," Jane suggested.

"Possibly," Louise said thoughtfully, "but I get quite a bit of background information before I agree to teach a new student, especially since I've decided to limit the number I take on. I like enough free time to help around the inn."

"You're such a good teacher. We don't want chores around here to interfere," Jane said with a concerned frown.

"Oh, they don't," Louise quickly assured her. "I love managing our bed-and-breakfast with both of you. Father would be proud of what we've done with this big old house."

"Without you to keep the books, we'd probably be up to our ears in red ink," Jane said with a chuckle.

She was notoriously uninterested in the finances of the inn, and she had the luxury of ignoring them because Louise was dedicated to keeping their ledgers.

"Well, I guess I'll find out tomorrow what Diana's mother wants. An invitation to tea sounds friendly, so a visit shouldn't involve a complaint about the lessons," Louise said.

"You know your pupils' parents appreciate you," Jane chided. "They're lucky to have you. There aren't many qualified piano teachers in the area, and none of your caliber. When you lived in Philadelphia, you had more students than you could handle."

"Well, it didn't hurt that my dear Eliot was a teacher too."

"The music world lost a gifted man when he passed away," Alice said in a tender voice.

Louise nodded and thought for a moment about her late husband. But right now it was Alice's unhappiness that concerned Louise, who fervently hoped that the little fawn would survive the night. She knew how it felt to be on sick watch. Her daughter Cynthia had given her some anxious moments when she was growing up, but thankfully all her childhood illnesses had been minor.

Louise knew she had to resist the temptation to check on the fawn herself. She very much wanted to open the shed door a crack just to make sure it was all right, but she accepted that this wouldn't in any way be helpful to the creature. She exchanged a telling glance with Jane, suspecting that her younger sister was fighting the same urge to look in on it.

"Maybe I'll try Mark's cell phone now," Alice said. "I know there's nothing he can do from Philadelphia, but I'd like to know whether we've handled the situation as well as we should have. Maybe there's some agency we could have called."

"I think Jack knows all the wildlife resources in our county," Louise said, sounding practical but not unsympathetic. "But it's a good idea to try calling Mark again."

Alice started to leave when the kitchen phone rang.

"I'll get it," Jane said, automatically reaching for it. "Grace Chapel Inn. Jane speaking."

She listened for a moment, and a broad smile creased her face.

"Good to hear from you. Just a minute, Mark. I'll get her."

She put her hand over the phone to muffle her voice. "It's Mark," she said unnecessarily.

"I'll take it at the registration desk," Alice said. "Then it will be easy to write down anything Mark tells me."

She hurried out of the kitchen while Jane held the phone. When she heard Alice's voice, she hung up.

"That's a relief," Louise said.

"I just hope Mark has something encouraging to say," Jane said.

"If I know Mark, he'll be kind and helpful."

Louise decided against going upstairs to her own room, at least until she heard what Alice's longtime friend had to say about their unexpected visitor.

As eager as she was to speak to Mark, Alice was apprehensive about explaining what they'd done with the fawn. She couldn't help but feel that there must be a better solution than putting it in their gardening shed.

"Alice, I got your message," he said when she picked up the phone and thanked him for calling. "It sounds like you have a problem."

The warmth in Mark's voice made her relax a little. He was never judgmental, and she could rely on him to be truthful and helpful. A long time ago in college, they'd been serious about each other but unable to get past the obstacles that stood between them. At that time Mark didn't have faith in the Lord. He'd grown up in a nonreligious home and couldn't understand how central Alice's beliefs were in her life. She was just beginning to prepare for her career as a nurse when he finished his veterinarian degree and embarked on travels that took him to faraway places from Antarctica to the Amazon, treating all manner of exotic animals. She never regretted that they'd taken separate paths, but she was glad that they'd renewed their friendship and was even happier that Mark had eventually accepted Christ and become a regular churchgoer in Philadelphia, where he now worked at the city's zoo.

He was still a handsome man, tall and slender with charcoal hair and a beard sprinkled with gray. Alice visualized him now as she tried to think of the best way to explain about the fawn.

"I hope I haven't done something foolish," she said.

"I can't imagine that you have."

Alice could hear the smile in his voice, and it encouraged her to tell the whole story.

"You do have a problem," Mark said after he'd heard her account of what had happened. "But under the circumstances, you did the only thing you could. The fawn had close to zero chance of surviving on its own once the mother was dead. The most important thing right now is that you don't try to feed it."

"We've left bottled water in a clean dish. That's all."

"Good. The thing to do tonight is leave it alone. I can't predict its chances of survival without seeing it, but we'll hope for the best."

"Louise and Jack cleared out the shed so nothing could endanger it, and Jane spread some soft branches as a bed."

"It sounds like you've all shown common sense, but if the fawn is as young as you think, you're going to need a special formula to feed it. You can give goat's or ewe's milk to a fawn, but not cow's. We use a manmade frozen colostrum at the zoo when it's needed. I can get some from our supplier for you."

"Should I drive there to get it?" Alice asked, willing to go to any length to provide for the fawn.

"I have a better idea. I'm driving to Cleveland tomorrow to give a speech for the zoo. I'll just leave a little earlier than planned, pick up the formula, keep it on ice in a cooler and make a side trip to Acorn Hill. It's not much out of my way, and I'll be happy to take a look at your fawn."

This was far more than Alice had expected, and she couldn't begin to tell him how grateful she was.

"It's been too long since I saw you," Mark said. "I'll look forward to it."

Alice found herself smiling after their conversation. She didn't often shift a burden onto other people, but she was relieved to know that Mark would examine the fawn and provide the means of feeding it. She was also pleased by the prospect of seeing her special friend.

She went back to the kitchen, eager to share the news with her sisters. Their problem was far from solved, but at least Mark's offer of help provided hope. They could face the other problems when the fawn's basic needs had been met. It would grow fast and couldn't be confined in a gardening shed for very long, but if it survived the night, the outlook would be much brighter.

"I can tell you have good news," Louise said as soon as she stepped into the kitchen.

As expected, both sisters were still there waiting to hear what Mark had said.

"Mark's coming himself tomorrow on his way to Cleveland," Alice reported. "He's going to bring a special formula so we can feed the fawn with a milk much like its mother would have provided. I can't tell you how relieved I am."

"I can tell that by looking at you," Jane said. "It's wonderful that he's driving here to examine the fawn."

"Fortunately, it's only a little out of his way. But it is a relief. I'm sure Dr. Ferris is a competent vet, but Mark has had such extensive experience with wild animals. He's sure to know what's best for the fawn."

"Then there's nothing we can do right now?" Louise asked.

"No, just pray that the poor little thing can make it through the night," Alice said.

"I hope you won't lie awake worrying all night," Jane said, hugging her sister. "You know, there's a small portion of tetrazzini left if you feel more like eating now."

Alice shook her head but expressed her thanks. "I'm still worried, but I'm more optimistic than I was."

"I think I'll call Viola," Louise said. "With her soft spot for animals, she's probably still up fretting just as we are."

"That would be nice of you," Alice agreed.

"I'll give Jack a buzz too," Jane said. "I'm sure he'll want to know. If you think about it, we're all sort of godparents to the little critter."

Chapter Four

*J*ane enjoyed being the first one up, with only Wendell to watch her prepare breakfast. The inn's cat typically pretended indifference to her activities, but he was quick to investigate any morsel she might accidentally drop. Unfortunately for him, there was nothing on the day's menu that would give him an impromptu treat.

On this Thursday morning Jane had gotten up especially early because their guests, the Larsens, wanted to be on the road before seven. Will and Maggie Larsen had stayed with them the previous fall on their way to an antiques show in Delaware and had made a special point of returning this spring. They were dealers from Michigan who made annual trips to a number of East Coast events.

The Larsens drove an RV, but on the outbound trip it was so loaded with their antiques stock that there wasn't room for them to sleep in it. Jane was delighted to have them. Their specialties were lamps, vintage toys and silver, but they were a font of information about all kinds of antiques. In fact, they had told her things that she hadn't known about the furnishings in Grace Chapel Inn. They especially admired the large Queen Anne mahogany table and the buffet in the dining room. They'd complimented the matching chairs, too, which especially pleased Jane. She loved the chair pads in subtle light green and ivory damask that went perfectly with the room's green walls. The Larsens predicted there would be a large demand for this type of revival furniture made in the 1920s. Will had wanted to check for a Grand Rapids label to see if it had been made in their home state, but his wife wouldn't let him.

"It's their home," she had rebuked him, apologizing for her husband because he got so wrapped up in his enthusiasm for antiques that he saw everything as potential stock.

Because they were leaving so early, Jane had opted for a simple meal of huevos rancheros. She prepared the mix of fresh tomatoes, green peppers and onions the day before, so all she had to do was heat it. As soon as the Larsens started down the stairs, Jane put servings of the hot vegetables on plates. Next she topped each with two fried eggs, sunny-side up, and added a garnish of toast points. Just to be sure her guests went off happy, she also served fruit compotes made from dried apricots, figs, peaches and pears topped with slivered almonds and served with hot-from-the-oven cornbread muffins.

"This is what I call eating," Will Larsen said as he broke apart a muffin and covered it with Jane's homemade orange marmalade.

"Will should know good food when he tastes it," Maggie said. "He's the cook at our house. You should see his cookbook collection. I bet he's got a hundred."

"More like thirty or forty," her husband said between bites.

Jane sat down at the table with them, always interested in conversation about cookbooks.

"Some include recipes from eighteenth-century Europe," Maggie said. "How they cooked in those days! A pinch of this, a dash of that."

"That's how I still cook," Will said with a grin. "Only without pounds of butter and lard."

"I should think not," his wife said. "You have to watch your cholesterol."

He agreed but broke the yolk on his second egg with obvious pleasure.

"I'm going to try to pick up some Amish cookbooks on this trip," Will said.

"I hope we sell more than he buys," Maggie said. "Some years it seems the RV is just as full when we get home as when we left."

"It sounds like fun," Jane mused. "I haven't been to an antiques show or flea market in ages. I buy most of the frames for my art that way and restore them myself. I'm nearly out of ones to work on."

"The spring antiquing season is just starting," Maggie said enthusiastically. "We won't touch home base again until just before the Fourth of July. Then we'll do a few shows closer to home."

"Once the weather gets good, we're gypsies," Will said, using his fork to capture some last bits of muffin.

"We talk about retiring, but we can't think of anything that's more fun than what we do now." Maggie laid her napkin beside the plate with part of her portion untouched. "It's delicious but more than I can finish, I'm afraid."

"Can't let it go to waste," her husband said, reaching over for her plate and placing his in front of his wife.

"Will! You don't need more," Maggie rebuked him.

"Nope, but this may be the best eating we get for weeks," he said with a sheepish grin.

Before the Larsens left, they booked a room for September when they would be doing a few shows west of Philadelphia. Jane enjoyed having them and looked forward to hearing more about their antiques business when they returned.

Her sisters hadn't come downstairs yet, and the Larsens had been their only guests the night before. That would change tomorrow. Coincidentally, two women from the Larsen's home state, Michigan, were scheduled to arrive for a longer stay, and the inn's four rooms were all booked for the weekend. In fact, there was even a waiting list in case anyone backed out at the last moment.

Now that her guests had departed, Jane worried again about what she and her sisters would see this morning when they opened the door to the shed. She hated the thought that all their efforts to save the fawn might have been futile.

Jane didn't want to be the one to open the shed door, but she had another idea. She hurried out to the shed, walking through grass still damp with dew. All the equipment that they'd hurriedly removed was scattered around the shed or leaning against the naturally aged wooden walls. She found what she needed, the sturdy stepladder that had served their needs for more years than Jane could remember. Unlike flimsy modern ones, it was built of thick hardwood, heavy to move but reassuringly safe to use. A history of the inn's interior could be read in the paint splashed on much of its surface. Jane could still see the rosy pink her father had painted her childhood room, and splatters of green from the dining room along with drips from every other wall in the house.

She carefully dragged it to a spot under the shed's one window, trying to be quiet so she wouldn't alarm the fawn. The building was low enough that she could see in the only opening by standing on the third rung of the ladder, as high as she cared to climb. From that vantage point, she could lean forward, bracing her hands on the window frame.

There was just enough morning light to allow Jane to make out the form of the fawn. It was sitting, head erect. She took a deep breath, hoping against hope that the still pose didn't bode ill. Then, to her immense relief, the fawn moved its head. It was alive.

"Jane, what are you doing?"

"Oh, Alice!" She was startled even though she'd half-expected her sister to check on the fawn as soon as she woke up. "I didn't want to open the door and scare the poor thing."

"Instead you're scaring me, teetering on top of that shaky old ladder."

"It's sturdy enough where I'm standing," Jane said, although she was happy to descend from the somewhat precarious perch.

"What did you see?" Alice asked, her sister's reckless-ness forgotten.

"The fawn is sitting up and moving its head," she reported. "Other than that, I couldn't see much."

"I wonder if we should open the door, just to be sure it has water."

"Do you think?" Jane was perfectly willing to let the decision be Alice's.

"Just a peek." Alice was already releasing the latch.

With Jane at her shoulder, she eased the door open a crack. "What do you see?"

The door creaked as Alice pushed it farther. She froze, and Jane nearly collided with her in her eagerness to see what Alice was seeing.

"I don't think she's touched the water," Alice said with distress.

"I wonder how long a wild baby can survive without it."

"Mark probably won't be here until after noon. His conference doesn't start until tomorrow, and he has to get what we need to feed it before he leaves Philadelphia."

"I'll feel a lot better when he's examined it," Jane admitted. "We're a little out of our league here."

"How can we get it to drink?" Jane could think of several possible ways, but she didn't feel confident about any of them.

"We need to go for some baby bottles when the grocery store opens, but I'd like to see it drink a little right now. We don't know how long a fawn can go without water."

"There must be some way to get water into its mouth without hurting it," Jane said hesitantly.

"Jack squeezed a little water into its mouth with his handkerchief, but I doubt that the fawn got more than a drop or two that way."

"We could use my baster," Jane said, thinking of the long tubelike implement with a rubber bulb that she used to baste turkeys or roasts.

"I guess if we're very careful." Alice's medical expertise made her uncomfortable with the thought of using a kitchen tool. "We'd have to be careful not to choke it with more water than it can swallow."

"It could be five or six hours before Mark gets here," Jane estimated. "That's a long time without water. Do you want to try it?"

"I guess." Alice sounded hesitant.

"You'll want to do it yourself, of course," Jane said, deferring to her sister's long experience caring for human patients.

Gathering the baster, bottled water and a clean bowl from the kitchen was the easy part. Jane followed Alice back to the shed, hanging back in the doorway while her sister stooped in front of the fawn.

"Do deer bite?" Jane said.

"Oh, I think not," Alice was quick to say. "They fight with their antlers. I guess I wouldn't want to collide with an adult's hoof, but I don't think our baby has an aggressive bone in his body."

"Or *her* body, if we're lucky. I can't imagine what we would do with a yearling buck. I wonder how old a fawn should be before it can be released into the wilderness."

"If ever," Alice whispered as she slowly moved the plastic tip to the fawn's mouth.

She squeezed only a tiny bit at a time, finally sighing with satisfaction when a small amount actually went into the delicate pink mouth instead of running down to the floor. The fawn's large, dark eyes peered up at her, as though they were begging her to restore the lost mother.

"What are you two doing?" Louise asked softly, approaching Jane as she stood in the partially open door.

"It's alive," Jane reported. "Alice is trying to get it to take a little water. We need to get some baby bottles as soon as the store is open."

"That's good news anyway." Louise peered into the shed to confirm for herself that the fawn had made it through the night.

"I'll go in and fix your breakfast," Jane said, assured that Alice had the situation under control.

"I can do it myself if you're needed here."

"That's okay. I don't think there's much to be done until Mark gets here."

She followed Louise into the kitchen, glad to occupy herself with familiar tasks. Life at the inn was never dull, but fawn rescue was a whole new experience.

After breakfast, Louise called Viola to tell her the latest news about the baby deer. Their conversation was brief because the bookstore owner was just leaving for Nine Lives, but she was grateful for the update.

"It's a relief to know a vet will be looking in on our fawn," Viola said.

Louise smiled at "our fawn," but in truth, she felt the same way. They'd rescued the poor little thing, so for better or worse, it was their responsibility.

She'd just ended her conversation with Viola when Louise received another call. It was Diana Zale's mother, inviting Louise to come for tea that afternoon.

Her two conversations left just enough time to get ready for her lesson with Diana, but Louise was a bit distracted by Mrs. Zale's invitation. Louise hoped it didn't mean that her daughter wouldn't be continuing her lessons. Diana was a talented student, and she'd already demonstrated an eagerness to learn that could take her a long way. Louise was planning a course of study for her that included work on some concert pieces in the near future. While Louise enjoyed working with children at all skill levels, it was particularly exciting to have students with the potential to excel.

The parlor was Louise's favorite room. It was spacious enough for her baby grand piano without crowding an assortment of Victorian furnishings that included three

Eastlake chairs, curio cabinets and a carved burl walnut table. While none of the Howard sisters thought of themselves as collectors, they did cherish antiques from their family's past. A collection of nineteenth- and early twentieth-century dolls was displayed on the table, most in original clothing and wigs with the best dolls displayed under glass domes. Their aunt Ethel, their father's half sister, had explained that little girls fortunate enough to receive china head dolls were encouraged to admire them rather than to play with them. Their grandmother's dolls were still in pristine condition because they'd sat on a shelf in the original boxes, largely untouched by her childish hands.

The vase collection included American art pottery in lovely shades of green, gold and rose, particular favorites of Jane. Louise especially liked a pair of Canton vases with Chinese scenes in oval panels. Alice favored simple country pieces like the terra-cotta pitcher their mother had once used to water plants. Now they kept it safe on a shelf, believing that it had formerly been used by a great-great-grandmother.

Louise removed the violet-and-ivory piano shawl and folded the silky fabric to set it aside during the lesson. According to the brass-faced clock on the fireplace mantel, her pupil was due in minutes. If Diana had one fault as a student, it was a tendency to rush in at the last moment or arrive a bit late. She was always apologetic, but Louise would have liked a more sedate beginning to their lessons. Still, Diana's enthusiasm more than made up for the hurried beginnings. Louise could forgive a lot when she had a pupil so eager to learn.

Diana usually came after school, but this Thursday she had a conflict. Louise was willing to be flexible on lesson times, and she appreciated Diana's initiative in rescheduling. She'd been excused from a study hall and had received permission to arrange for transportation to and from the inn.

True to form, Diana rushed into the parlor a couple of minutes late and took awhile to extract her music from an overloaded black backpack. She was dressed for school in jeans and a boysenberry knit shirt with lace edging around the V-neck. Her thick-soled running shoes boosted her height to a little over five feet. Her silky honey-brown hair was long and straight, and she always tucked it behind her ears before she started to play. She was a pretty girl with luminous hazel eyes and lips that formed an O when she concentrated on her music.

Louise liked to exchange a few pleasantries with her students before they began their lessons, but this morning she immediately started Diana on her scales. She would have to watch the clock to keep her from being late for her next class.

As soon as she began her first piece, it was obvious that Diana had practiced as much as any teacher could expect. Her hands looked delicate, but her slender fingers were agile, rippling over the keys with confidence.

"I can tell that you worked hard on that," Louise complimented her student.

The lesson time passed quickly, and she decided against asking Diana any questions about her mother's invitation to tea. Whatever Mrs. Zale wanted to discuss, she obviously preferred to do it in the privacy of her home. Louise would have to curb her curiosity until the afternoon.

Alice knew that nothing made time pass more slowly than keeping an eye on the clock. She deliberately found a few outdoor jobs to keep her mind off the fawn.

The morning was cool, but the sun was bright. By the time Alice finished sweeping the long front porch, she felt overheated. The shed would get hot by midday, and she didn't know how that would affect the fawn. She fervently hoped Mark would arrive early to give his expert advice.

Noon came, and Jane urged her to come inside for a light lunch: spinach salad with Jane's cheesy breadsticks. She'd made extra, anticipating that Mark might join them, but he didn't arrive while they were eating. The three sisters lingered at the table, and Louise speculated about her invitation to tea at the Zales' home. Alice tried to concentrate on the conversation, but she was thinking about Mark's arrival.

His visits were always welcome, Alice admitted to herself. There was a warmth and depth in their rekindled friendship that added a new dimension to her life. He was the same man she'd known so many years ago, but he'd matured into a kind, caring human being who took life much more seriously than he once had. She was especially happy for his sake that he was embarked on his own quest for faith. It was gradually forming a new kind of bond between them, a fellowship of believers.

In many ways Mark hadn't changed. He still had a great zest for learning, and he loved to travel. Although he was a little older than Alice, he wasn't eager to retire anytime soon. The quiet life that Alice loved in Acorn Hill wouldn't suit his energetic habits, at least not yet. She accepted his friendship with the wisdom of a mature woman, not wanting to change any of the things that made him special.

Alice wanted to freshen up. She went up to her room, assured that Jane would keep an eye out for Mark. She washed and slipped into clean khaki walking shorts and a pale peach knit top that brought out the reddish highlights in her hair. She wasn't exactly dressing up for Mark, but she didn't want to greet him in yard clothes.

With time on her hands until Mark arrived, she resisted the urge to check on the fawn. She would leave ladder climbing to Jane and wait until Mark was there to open the door with her. As a nurse, she practiced do-no-harm caregiving, and it seemed sensible to wait for a vet's expert instructions before taking any action.

Jane had made a trip to the grocery store and secured an assortment of baby bottles, anticipating that they would have to feed the fawn with those items. Louise needed to do some errands before she went to the Zales' for tea, but she'd promised to help in any way she could with the care and feeding. Both Viola and Jack were probably waiting to hear Mark's verdict. Alice smiled, realizing that she had a whole team of concerned animal lovers to help her.

Once downstairs, she paced the entryway and kitchen until Jane shooed her away.

"Go read one of your mysteries," her younger sister insisted. "There's absolutely nothing that you need to be doing right now."

Rather than be in the way, Alice retrieved a book she'd started several days before and retreated to the front porch to enjoy reading it in her favorite wicker lounge chair. It was warm but not uncomfortably hot as she settled down to try to outguess the sleuth in the story. After a few pages, she realized that the book was rather disappointing. Her eyelids grew heavy, and she had a hard time concentrating.

"You have the face of an angel when you're asleep."

Alice woke with a start to find Mark standing in front of her with a broad smile on his weathered but still handsome face.

"Oh, Mark, I must have drifted off. Did you just get here?"

"Just this minute. It's good to see you, Alice."

He offered his hand to help her from the chair, and she smiled her thanks.

"Have you had lunch? Jane made a nice spinach salad."

"I stopped on the road, thank you."

Alice glanced at her watch, surprised that it was past two o'clock. She'd napped longer than she thought.

"I can't tell you how grateful I am for your help. We all are. It feels like such a big responsibility to care for a helpless creature. I hope we did the right thing bringing it here."

"If the mother was dead, you made the only possible choice. Since most fawns are born in May around here, it's probably much too young to survive on its own. How about if I take a look at it?"

"Of course, that's why you came. As I told you, it's in the gardening shed in back, the only place we could think to put it. Jack O'Hara, our friend who's an animal control officer, said that dogs are the worst fawn predators in this area. I don't think many neighbors let theirs run loose, but I wanted a safe temporary haven."

She noticed that Mark had a small black case with him and felt even more reassured that the fawn had professional help. He was dressed casually, obviously ready to minister to the young animal. She led the way to the shed, walking around the outside of the large cocoa-brown Victorian house with Mark beside her.

"I'll go inside the shed alone," he said as they reached the door. "The fewer humans the fawn has to deal with, the better."

Alice stayed back from the doorway. She could hear Mark murmuring to the animal but couldn't see what he was doing.

"It's a female," he called out to her in a muted voice just loud enough for her to hear.

Her mind registered that as a good thing.

"Has she had any water?" he asked in the same low, soothing voice.

"We tried to give her some bottled water with Jane's baster. I think she got a little but not much. Jane bought some baby bottles, but we wanted you to see her before we tried again."

Mark seemed to be spending an awfully long time with the fawn, but Alice was grateful that he was being thorough.

She very much hoped that he would pronounce her in good condition.

At last he came out carrying his case.

"She's doing well considering the loss of her mother. If you can get her to take nourishment, I think she'll make it. I have frozen colostrum in a cooler in the car, enough to last several days. I'll take care of getting more when you need it. The bad news is that you can't keep her in the shed indefinitely. She will need to be in a controlled outdoor situation where she can eventually learn to graze for food."

"When she can get food herself, can she be released into the wild?"

Mark's expression wasn't reassuring.

"After the human contact that it takes to feed and care for her, she might not have the survival skills she needs in the wild. Humans are a deer's worst enemy. This one won't realize that after being hand-fed."

"What should we do then?"

"For now, just worry about getting her to eat. Then you need to find a better situation. When she's able to fend for herself, I have a few ideas about where she can go. I'll have to do some checking and get back to you. I'm afraid I don't pay as much attention as I should to local wildlife. A sick rhino or a rogue baboon is more in my line of work."

"So for now all we can do is try to feed her. Will she be all right in the shed on warm days?"

"Should be. I see you opened the window. That's good."

"Jack O'Hara is going to look into a better temporary place to keep her, maybe a farm."

"That would be an improvement over the shed. Meanwhile, I'll bring the cooler inside so you can put the colostrum in your freezer. Just thaw what you intend to use right away. Bring it to room temperature in the microwave. It's not so different from feeding a human baby."

"I guess we can manage that." Alice smiled.

"Oh, before I forget, I have a bale of hay in the back of my van. The cuttings were a fair substitute, but you're going to want to spread some hay and change it frequently. I printed out some instructions from the Internet. They're from a fawn rescue organization and will give you some of the basics."

"Thank you so much, Mark," Alice said. "This is a new challenge for all of us. Can I offer you some coffee or tea?"

"I would really like a glass of Jane's iced tea," he said with a familiar smile. "I just wish I could stick around for a while to see how your new guest gets on. But I made this speaking commitment a year ago. I can't back out at the last minute."

"Of course not. I'm only so grateful that you came and brought the formula."

"What are friends for?" He smiled with his whole face, his eyes sparkling with a mixture of good humor and concern. "I wouldn't say no to Jane's cookies if she happens to have some on hand."

"She wouldn't be Jane if she didn't."

Alice's spirit lifted as Mark talked and joked with Jane and her over a plate of Jane's frosted lemon bars, Mark's favorite treat, which she'd baked up fresh that morning in anticipation of his visit. He kidded that he would have come without the incentive of seeing the fawn if he'd known she was making them.

Alice was always sorry to see Mark leave, but she regretted it even more this time. Somehow they had to make sure the fawn accepted the substitute for its mother's milk that Mark had delivered. Otherwise they would surely lose her. She didn't even want to think about failure.

Chapter Five

The Zales lived on the outskirts of Acorn Hill in an area built up in the last ten years. The homes were mostly two stories and reminded Louise of farmhouses of an earlier era. The Zales' house had pale-yellow vinyl siding with white trim. An oversized garage was attached to the house, and a small front porch had several baskets of plants hanging above the railing. The shrubs in front were small and carefully manicured, and the grass had been recently mowed. It was a well-tended home, one that showed pride of ownership.

She went up four steps to the porch and smiled at a pair of skateboards sitting beside the door. Diana had mentioned having two younger brothers. She pushed a buzzer, and the door was opened almost immediately.

"Mrs. Smith, it's so nice of you to come." Mrs. Zale stood back to let her guest enter.

She was pretty and petite like Diana, but she seemed a little older than Louise had expected. Perhaps it was a certain careworn look that added years or the fact that her brown hair was liberally laced with gray. She was dressed in a blue denim skirt with a red knit top, and when she smiled there was natural warmth in her pale blue eyes. Louise liked her right away.

"It's my pleasure. And please call me Louise." She stepped onto the flagstones in the foyer.

"I'll try to remember. Diana talks about you so often that it's hard not to think of you as Mrs. Smith."

Louise was flattered but surprised. It never occurred to her that students would talk about her unless quizzed about lessons by their parents.

"I hope you'll call me Lara," her hostess said, leading the way through an understated living room furnished with large framed pictures of Diana and her two brothers, who looked to be around ten and twelve. The dining area was bursting with color. Several large wreaths made of natural material like straw and willow branches were festooned with huge violet and orange bows. Small floral watercolors were grouped on one wall, and another held framed arrangements of dried flowers.

"My hobbies," Lara explained with a self-deprecating laugh. "My husband likes things neat and uncluttered, so I keep the living room that way for him. I spill all over the rest of the house, and the kids hang out mostly in the family room off the kitchen. That's where we keep Diana's piano."

"This room is delightful," Louise said sincerely.

"Thank you. Everything is ready," Lara said. "Diana told me that you're never late. Please, have a seat while I get the tea."

The table setting was charming, and Louise was quick to compliment her hostess. A fine lace tablecloth was set with bone china cups, saucers and plates. The floral designs featured violets and looked hand painted, each piece rimmed with gold trim. A silver tea set dominated the table and included a tray that held finger sandwiches and short-bread cookies.

"I hope you like watercress sandwiches," Lara said as she put the teapot on the tray. "My grandmother was English. She taught me how to make them along with plum pudding and beef Wellington. My family prefers things like spaghetti and pizza, so I don't often use her recipes."

"I love watercress sandwiches, but it's been ages since I had any," Louise said with enthusiasm. "You'll have to meet my sister Jane. She's a professional chef and does all the cooking for Grace Chapel Inn. She would love to trade recipes with you."

"That would be nice, although I don't get into town very often."

Louise was a bit surprised at this admission but didn't want to ask why. The Zales only lived a mile or so from the center of Acorn Hill, far enough for the children to ride the school bus but certainly not a great distance.

The watercress sandwiches were a treat, the leaves fine-chopped and mixed in with rich cream cheese; and the homemade cookies were delightful.

"This is really lovely, Lara. I can't thank you enough for asking me."

"I should have gotten to know Diana's teacher sooner. I do feel a bit guilty, though."

"Whatever for?" Louise wondered if her first suspicion was true. Had Lara invited her here to cancel Diana's lessons?

"I have a favor to ask, a really big favor. I have no right to impose on you, but Diana loves her lessons with you. She's never had such a gifted teacher. In fact, this was partly her idea."

Louise's head was buzzing with possibilities. Did Diana want to have her lessons at home? Louise preferred that students come to her, but she might be willing to make an exception for a gifted pupil like Diana. She took a sip of the excellent Earl Grey tea and kept silent.

"The truth is, I'm narcoleptic."

She paused. Louise felt she had to say something, although she couldn't see where this admission was going.

"I'm so sorry."

"I take medication, of course," Lara continued. "It's fairly effective, but the bottom line is that the condition keeps me from driving. I never learned. I've always been afraid of falling asleep behind the wheel. It can happen so suddenly that I might be a danger on the road."

"That must be such a problem when you have children."

"Yes, they always need to go somewhere. It wasn't so difficult with my husband's old job before we moved here, but now he has to travel quite a bit. The boys like to be involved in sports. Diana has so many activities at the school. It's become a serious problem."

"Diana—"

"She's seventeen, old enough to be driving, I know. Her father even bought a used car for her to drive. It will be an immense help when she can take her brothers to the places they need to go, not to mention getting places herself. The trouble is, she can't get her license."

"She'll be able to get it after she takes driver education, won't she?"

"She took driver education through the school where we used to live. She's also taken lessons from a private driving school. Her father tried too." Lara shook her head sadly. "She hasn't been able to pass the driving test. She does fine on the written part, but she falls apart on the road test."

"Surely she can retake it?"

"Diana's failed twice. She's afraid to try again."

"That's a shame. She's such a quick learner." Louise was still mystified as to why Lara was telling her this.

"She learns fast from you because you're such a good teacher."

"Well, thank you. She's doing very well with her lessons."

"I have to tell you the whole truth. The teacher giving her private lessons made her so nervous that she turned a corner and hit a parked car. The accident totally destroyed what little confidence she had. I desperately need her to be able to drive, but she's balked at practicing, even with her father. Well, especially her father. He can't understand why she's having so much trouble."

"That's a shame."

Louise had a bad feeling about where this was headed, but she listened patiently, sympathizing with young Diana's struggle to master driving skills.

"Diana thinks she could pass her driver's test if she had a good teacher like you to help her."

"Perhaps a counselor at the high school could recommend someone. Or I could ask around. My sister Alice's best friend is a teacher. Maybe between them they could help."

"Oh dear, I haven't explained this at all well. The truth is, Diana wants you to give her driving lessons. We would be happy to pay you well for as many sessions as it takes to get her license."

"I'm really not qualified," Louise said, taking a deep breath and trying to let Lara down easily. "I teach music because I love it. But driving..."

"It's not like you would be starting with basic skills. She knows what to do. She just doesn't have the confidence."

"It's really not my field," Louise said weakly.

"You could use our car for the lessons. And Diana understands that she has to be willing to drive at any time that's convenient for you."

"She would be better off with a professional driver-education teacher."

Lara shook her head sadly. "No, you really are her last chance."

"Surely, I can't be." Louise felt terrible about refusing to help, but it was such a bizarre idea, her teaching a teen to drive.

"Please don't say no now. At least give it some thought," Diana's mother urged. "If you don't have the time, we'll understand. It won't affect her piano lessons. But you would be doing us a tremendous favor."

"I'll certainly think about it," Louise reluctantly agreed.

She thanked Lara for the lovely tea and left as soon as she could without seeming to rush away.

Driving lessons! She could have been flattered by Diana's confidence in her, but she couldn't imagine giving lessons to a young girl who had already failed her driving test twice. What could Louise possibly tell her that other teachers hadn't? She wouldn't have a clue how to begin. There was a world of difference between mastering a musical instrument and controlling a car. Pianos didn't sideswipe other pianos.

$\backsim$

"I'm at my wit's end," Alice said as she came into the kitchen through the side entrance. "The poor thing must be close to starving, but she refuses to suckle. I know formula in a baby bottle isn't the same as her mother's milk, but a fawn must be born with enough survival instincts to accept a substitute when her life is at stake."

"Oh, dear thing," Jane sympathized. "Aunt Ethel and I were just having some iced tea. Why don't you have a glass with us?"

"Oh, hello, Aunt Ethel. I'm so concerned about the fawn that I didn't even notice you."

Alice managed to smile although she was too worried to participate in the chitchat that her aunt enjoyed. She was fond of her father's half sister and was glad that she lived in the carriage house beside the inn, but Alice wasn't in the mood for town gossip.

"How do you like Aunt Ethel's new blouse?" Jane asked, perhaps to change the subject that they'd been discussing when Alice came in.

"Very pretty," Alice said automatically, scarcely glancing at the gaily patterned blue-and-gold garment.

"You don't think it makes me look just a tiny bit plump?" her aunt asked with concern.

Ethel was a little plump. Alice sometimes thought of her affectionately as a little dumpling, although she was far from pale with her lively blue eyes and vivid red hair.

"Are you sure the fawn didn't take any nourishment at all?" Jane asked after pouring a tall glass of mint tea for her sister.

"Afraid so. I'll try again in a little while."

"Jane told me about the fawn," Ethel said. "They usually die without a mother. Maybe you shouldn't have brought it here."

Jane groaned softly, and Alice launched into a justification for their rescue attempt.

"You'll lose it if you can't get it to eat," Ethel pointed out.

Her aunt's pronouncement didn't make Alice feel any better, although she was all too aware of the grim consequences if the fawn continued to refuse the bottle.

"We had orphan animals on the farm once in a while. That was back when Bob and I were young," Ethel said. "We had all kinds of animals in those days—cows, pigs, chickens, geese, sheep, even a few goats. Of course, today farmers like to specialize. Grow just one or two crops and not bother with livestock unless they do it in a big way. I wouldn't have wanted one of those modern hog barns on our farm. I was glad when Bob phased out the animals except for some beef cattle."

Alice had a hard time concentrating on her aunt's reminiscences, most of which she'd heard numerous times, but one word had caught her attention.

"What kind of orphans?" she asked.

"I had a lamb or two in my kitchen several times. Lost the mothers birthing, so we had to keep them inside for a while in a warm place. My boys really liked having a lamb as a temporary pet. They'd fix up a big cardboard box as a pen. We had a couple of goats too, tiny little things. I thought we'd lose one of them for sure, but it pulled through."

"Did you bottle-feed your orphans?" Alice asked.

"Yes, I remember Bob had to get some special formula. Usually they took it from a baby bottle, but once I had to use a doll-sized bottle."

"Did any of them refuse to nurse from a bottle?" Alice asked with a growing sense of urgency.

"One of the kids did, as I recall. That's a baby goat, you know. I remember that I watched this program on TV. I can't remember what it was now, but in the story they had a calf that wouldn't take a bottle. Maybe it was one of those Western shows. My Bob used to like Roy Rogers, Gene Autry, all those cowboys. No, I don't think it was one of their shows. But it was definitely from the television that I got the idea for our kid."

Alice curbed her impatience. Ethel would tell her story in her own way. Experience told her that there was no rushing her aunt's memories.

"What idea?" Jane asked.

"You know, to feed the baby goat."

"Yes, but how did you do it?" Alice had to ask.

"An old farming trick. I poked a small hole in one of the fingers of a rubber glove, then poured some formula into it. No, I think Bob got some goat's milk from another farmer. It surprised me, but our kid took to it. Probably it seemed more like its mother than the bottle nipples did. I'm proud to say that we never lost an animal that I took into my kitchen."

"That's a wonderful idea, Aunt Ethel," Jane said, giving Alice a look that asked whether she would like to try it.

Alice nodded. She was willing to try anything that might save her fawn.

Louise returned to find a gathering in the kitchen. Jane was sitting at the table with her wicker box of sewing supplies, while Alice and Ethel hovered over her shoulder. Jane had a long, wicked-looking needle in one hand and a rubber glove in the other.

"What are you doing?" Louise asked.

"The fawn won't feed from a bottle," Jane explained. "Aunt Ethel suggested we try puncturing the finger of a rubber glove."

"It worked on the farm when we had an orphan kid— kid goat, that is—that wouldn't suckle from a baby bottle," she said.

"Let me test it with water," Jane said, getting up and walking to the sink.

Everyone was quiet while she experimented with the glove finger.

"It works. The fawn shouldn't have any trouble getting formula through this hole."

"If she'll accept it," Alice said.

"There's only one way to find out," Jane said. "Alice, do you want to try it?"

"I want to watch," their aunt said. "It's been quite a few years since I had to hand-feed a baby animal."

"Okay, but Alice should go into the shed alone," Jane said emphatically. "The rest of us can watch through the doorway, but we'd better stay back. We don't want to overwhelm the poor little thing."

Louise forgot her news for the moment and followed her sisters and aunt out to the gardening shed. Alice filled the finger with formula from the rejected bottle before going inside, then knelt beside the fragile-looking fawn.

"Hasn't she stood up at all?" Louise asked in a soft voice.

"No," Jane said. "She's been hunkered down every time we looked at her. Either she's still terrified, or she's too weak to get up."

"A good meal should perk her up," Ethel said in a tone of authority.

She pressed forward to see what Alice was doing, but Louise gently touched her arm to keep her back.

Alice held the swollen finger of the glove to the fawn's mouth. At first it appeared that the little creature was indifferent to her offering. Then Alice's shoulders visibly relaxed.

"She's taking it," Alice said in a husky whisper that barely carried to their ears.

"What did she say?" Ethel asked.

"The fawn has started to nurse," Jane said.

"Praise the Lord!" Ethel said, forgetting to mute her voice.

"Your idea saved the fawn, Aunt Ethel," Jane said, giving her aunt a spontaneous hug.

"You don't get to be my age without learning a trick or two." She grinned with satisfaction.

Louise smiled at that. Their aunt was secretive about her age, not even willing to admit that she was a senior citizen—except when it came to seeking the seniors' discount in restaurants. Their father had passed away at the age of ninety-two, but Ethel was considerably younger. Still, she had to be well into her seventies, something she tried to conceal by keeping her hair a vibrant shade of red and dressing in bright, cheerful outfits. Today she was wearing a long cobalt-blue skirt with her new blouse. Louise suspected that Ethel sometimes took her fashion cues from the covers of the romance novels she read so avidly.

When Alice was satisfied that the fawn was finished, she locked the door of the shed and went with them to the kitchen.

"You'll stay for dinner, won't you, Aunt Ethel?" Jane asked.

"You're not having anything with broccoli, are you? I've decided that it doesn't agree with me too well."

"No broccoli," Jane assured her. "We're having beef-and-mushroom oriental on a mix of long-grain and wild rice. It will be ready as soon as I cook the rice."

"Well, in that case—"

"Good," said Jane. Their aunt liked to be coaxed a bit before she consented to join them, although Louise couldn't remember her ever refusing an invitation unless she had special plans.

"You're the heroine of the day, Aunt Ethel," Alice said. "Without your idea about the glove, I don't know what we would have done."

Louise went up to her room to change into a comfortable skirt and a loose-fitting shirt that buttoned down the front. Mostly she wanted a few minutes to think before joining her family for dinner.

Lord, she prayed silently, *help me to make the right decision about Diana. I don't feel qualified to teach driving, but I can see that Lara is distressed by her condition and needs help. If Diana is such a poor driver that she doesn't belong behind the wheel of a car, will I be doing a great disservice by helping her get her license? Please guide me in making the right decision.*

She felt a little better when she rejoined her sisters and aunt in the kitchen, but her decision was still hanging in the air. She wasn't at all sure that she could teach Diana what she needed to know after other instructors had failed.

Louise kept her own counsel during dinner, which they shared around the kitchen table. Ethel kept the conversation going with all the newsy items she'd garnered since their last family gathering. Louise listened but ate little, blaming her sluggish appetite on the tea treats that Lara Zale had prepared. She wanted to discuss Diana's driving problems with her sisters but decided to wait until Ethel went home for the evening. She loved her somewhat flighty relative, but she didn't want the Zales' problems to become fodder for town gossip. Louise liked people to respect her privacy, and she treated her students' confidences with utmost respect.

Ethel left soon after dinner because she wanted to watch a favorite television show. Jane gave her the remainder of the lemon bars that had been served as dessert, putting them on a plate and covering them with plastic wrap.

"She really did help us this time," Alice said with affection.

Her sisters nodded, and Jane mimicked a clapping of hands.

"There's something I want to talk over with you if you have time," Louise said.

"When do we not have time for you?" Alice asked, her eyebrows raised in surprise.

"Never," Louise admitted. "It's about the Zales."

"I remember that you were a little puzzled about the invitation to tea," Jane said.

"It was a lovely tea, but Diana has a problem. She's taken driver education and private lessons, but she hasn't been able to pass the driving test to get her license. Her mother wants me to try teaching her."

"To drive?" Alice sounded as surprised as Louise had been when she first heard it. "But why you? Not that you're not a good driver, but it sounds like risky business to me. Don't driver-training cars have a separate brake for the teacher?"

"It's Diana's idea. She likes her music lessons and thinks I could help her with driving as well."

"You told her no, didn't you?" Jane asked.

"Not exactly. I said that I would think about it."

"You're not actually considering it, are you?" Alice rarely turned down a request for help herself, but she obviously thought the Zales' request was unreasonable.

"Diana isn't just another teen who would like to be able to drive. Her mother is narcoleptic. She can't drive, and she has two younger boys who need to be taken places on a regular basis. It would be immensely helpful if Diana could take them to their activities. Her father travels a lot. In fact, he's already bought a second car for Diana to use, but she hasn't been able to pass the driving part of the license test."

"My, that puts things in a different perspective," said Alice.

"Can you find the time to do it?" Jane asked.

"Will it be too stressful for you?" Alice wanted to know.

"I can find time to try a few lessons," Louise said thoughtfully. "Whether I should is another question. I have my pupils to consider, not to mention the work around here. Our rooms are booked well into the summer.

"Oh, that reminds me," Jane said. "We did have a cancellation. One of the Michigan women has a family crisis, but her friend is still coming. She'll be here tomorrow, but that leaves us with one empty room. I'll call someone on our waiting list this evening. But don't worry about the work. As long as you keep the books, you're doing more than your share. I loathe bookkeeping."

Her sisters laughed at her vehemence, although they knew it wasn't an exaggeration. Jane had never had the patience for meticulous accounting.

"You could agree to a certain number of lessons, maybe two or three, and see how they go," Alice suggested. "If she's had a lot of training already, maybe all she needs is confidence."

"Or maybe she's simply not qualified to be behind the wheel of a car," Jane said.

"Either way, you'll know after a few sessions with her. You wouldn't continue piano lessons with a tone-deaf, hopeless student," said Alice.

"Like me," Jane said with a soft laugh.

"I think you have a good idea," Louise said with the relief that comes with a decision made. "I'll agree to two— no, three—lessons and see how they go."

There was no reason to keep the Zales in suspense now that her decision was made. Before she went up to her room for the evening, she used the phone at the registration desk to call Lara.

"I'm only agreeing to a few trial lessons, no more than three," Louise emphasized when Lara thanked her profusely. "By that time I'll know whether I can be of any help to Diana."

"I'll write a check for the three lessons right away," Lara said.

"No, I don't want to be paid," Louise insisted. "This is a service among friends. Diana is a wonderful piano student, and I know we can make good progress together in music. I have to be honest and tell you that I'm not nearly as confident about driving lessons. They'll be a learning experience for me too."

After she hung up, Louise hoped that she hadn't made a big mistake.

Chapter Six

*A*lice went out to the shed early on Friday morning, even before Jane had finished fixing breakfast for their guests. To her surprise and relief, the little fawn was standing on its fragile-looking legs.

"Well, baby, you're looking so much better this morning," Alice said in a soft, soothing voice.

Now that they knew the fawn was female, they should give her a name. Or should they? They were only temporary caregivers. The poor creature couldn't stay in their shed much longer. That building was only a wildlife version of an emergency room. Naming the fawn would only make it harder to give her up.

Alice set the basket she was carrying on the worktable, taking care to shut the door behind her. She could see herself in hot pursuit of a runaway fawn, a chase that she was unlikely to win. First she turned on a battery-operated lantern so she could see what she was doing in the gloom of the shed. The formula was thawed and ready to use as Mark had instructed. Alice had put it in one of the baby bottles in case the fawn was ready to accept a nipple.

She wasn't. Alice thought she could read fear in the fawn's eyes, and it made her even more determined to save the little creature.

It wasn't difficult to fill the finger of a rubber glove with the formula. The trick was to get it into the fawn's mouth before the liquid leaked out of the hole that Jane had punched. It did help that the little deer was standing, and Alice teased her mouth with the life-giving fluid until she took it.

It was gratifying to watch the fawn nurse, and Alice refilled the finger with the same happy results. She accidentally brushed the downy pelt with the back of her hand and marveled at the softness of the animal's protective coat. She wanted to hug the creature and comfort it, but the best thing she could do for it now was attend to its needs.

There was more to fawn care than feeding, though, and Alice had appointed herself to remove yesterday's bedding with a rake and replace it with fresh hay from the bundle Mark had left. If the fawn stayed with them much longer, she would have to find a supply of straw. It was a big if.

She wasn't sure what to do with the used bedding, so she donned Jane's gardening gloves and bagged it. Their trash service would probably take one extra bag that week, but they certainly might balk at hauling away bag after bag.

How long would she and her sisters play host to the orphan? Alice would talk to Jack O'Hara today. Maybe he had a lead on a place that would accept the animal.

The practical thing was to find a farm where the owners were wildlife enthusiasts, if such a place existed. It would still be hard to let her go. Alice's instinct was to adopt it as a pet and cherish it as she did the inn's cat, Wendell. Reason, however, told her that this wasn't in the best interest of the deer.

As she worked, Alice allowed herself to think of fanciful plans to keep the creature at Grace Chapel Inn. They could fence the garden area and have their own deer park. Of course, there wouldn't be a garden once the fawn learned to graze. Worse, it seemed cruel to confine a wild animal. She rejected the idea and steeled herself against the inevitable. The deer had to go. The question was where.

After she'd done all she could for the fawn, she went back to the kitchen to wash her hands, then told Jane that she was going for her morning walk before she ate.

"How's the fawn doing?" Jane asked.

"Standing up, although she seems a little unsteady. She still won't take the nipple, but she nursed well from the glove finger. I changed the bedding, so there's nothing for you to do."

"I'm glad to hear she's eating. The formula Mark gave you will build up her strength. Are you sure you don't want a cornbread muffin before your walk?"

"No, thanks. I'll have something when I get home."

"Louise isn't down yet. Maybe we can have breakfast together after the guests check out. I'm eager to meet the Michigan lady who's due this afternoon. She'll be here for some time, so I hope she's as pleasant as our last Michigan guests."

"Oh, the antiques dealers. I didn't really get to talk much with them."

"They are a treasury of information about antiques, and I'm happy to say they'll be coming again. They've already booked their next visit."

"It's your cooking that brings guests back again and again," Alice said with a broad smile.

She couldn't imagine running a bed-and-breakfast without Jane's wizardry in the kitchen. She and Louise might settle for a diet of cold cereal, sandwiches and TV dinners if they had to cook for themselves. Because Jane was such a superb cook, Alice was doubly conscientious about her brisk morning walks.

Fortunately, she loved getting out early and walking while Acorn Hill was quiet and peaceful, not that it was ever noisy or crowded. She would be glad when her walking partner Vera began her summer break from teaching at the elementary school so they could walk together more often.

Alice walked fast and made a circuit of the town center. Time went quickly because she was lost in thought, wondering what would happen to the fawn and whether Mark would stop on his way back to Philadelphia. She was glad they'd had his professional advice about caring for the fawn, but they still had to face the bigger problem of what to do with it. She considered other alternatives. They could put an ad in the newspaper or call local vets.

Her return route took her past the town hall and Viola's Nine Lives Bookstore. It was too early for the store to be open, but Alice stopped and checked out the books on display in the front window. Viola loved the classics, so it wasn't surprising to see an attractive lineup of leather-bound books, their titles embossed in gold lettering. She was having a special on Dickens and Austen, neither likely to be best sellers in Acorn Hill, but that didn't deter Viola from featuring them in her window. She ordered what the townsfolk liked to read, including the mysteries Alice bought from her, but her heart belonged to another realm.

Alice was about to leave when she caught a shadow of motion in the store interior. She tapped softly on the window, and Viola hurried to the door to let her in.

"I don't want to bother you, but I thought you might like an update on our fawn. She was standing up when I went to the shed this morning."

"That is good news," Viola said. "Come on in. I came to the store early because I was awake anyway. Have a cup of tea with me. I have a kettle heating in the back room."

"Thank you, I'd love to," she said.

They made their way past orderly arrangements of carefully selected books. Viola probably did more to promote good literature than all the English teachers in the county. Alice knew she would never have read Dostoyevsky's *Crime and Punishment* without Viola's enthusiastic recommendation, and she was grateful that she had. It raised her expectations in reading the mysteries she loved.

The back room was crowded. Books overflowed their shelves and were piled up on tables and the floor. Viola had recently set herself up to sell antiquarian books online, a business that was close to her heart. A small portion of the room contained her battered oak desk, computer, files and a pair of office chairs. A coffeemaker and a bakery box stood on a tea cart that had seen better days.

"I hope you'll have a scone," Viola said, offering Alice one of the rich triangular pastries that were a specialty of the Good Apple Bakery in town.

"I'd love one. I went off without breakfast, and now I'm famished."

Viola's tea was hot and strong, and it filled the room with its fragrance. Alice enjoyed it from the first sip.

"So tell me, how is our fawn doing?"

"We had a feeding problem, but Aunt Ethel gave us an idea that worked for her when she had orphan lambs and kids on her farm. The fawn wouldn't take a nipple, so we're feeding it through the finger of a rubber glove."

"That is clever," Viola acknowledged. "Lost creature. I had trouble getting to sleep last night thinking about its mother."

"Yes, I know how you feel. I remember crying the first time I saw *Bambi*. I was pretty young, but I thought it was so unfair that the mother was killed."

"I couldn't see it today without feeling the same way," Viola admitted.

"Have the kittens come yet?" Alice asked, remembering Viola's urgency to get home to her expectant feline.

"Not yet, but it could be any minute. I thought of bringing the mother-to-be here for the day, but she's a secretive little mommy. She probably has her nesting place all picked out. I don't want to distress her by taking her away from it."

"Our problem now is to find a place to raise the fawn until it's old enough to survive on its own," Alice said between bites of the luscious scone. "Now that she's standing, I can see how quickly she'll outgrow our shed."

"Yes, you'll have to find new quarters for her soon," Viola agreed with a flip of the bright white-and-gold scarf she was wearing today with a long purple skirt and her dusting smock of sunny yellow cotton.

"It might be easier if we lived out in the country," Alice mused.

"Like the people in *The Yearling* by Marjorie Kinnan Rawlings," Viola said. "They were farmers in the scrublands of Florida, if I remember correctly."

"I don't think I ever read the book, but I remember that it was made into a movie a long time ago."

"Nineteen forty-six," Viola said. "I looked it up on the computer. If I can find a copy, I'd like to reread the book now that we've had a fawn experience ourselves. I don't think it had a happy ending for the deer, though. In the movie it ate the poor farmer's crops, and his son had to sacrifice it for his family."

"Oh dear," Alice said, "I hope our fawn's story has a happy ending. I'm afraid I've gotten attached to her already."

"You have a tender heart." Her friend smiled and refilled their cups. "Of course, life rarely has the neat, clean endings that most books do. Maybe that's why I love books so much. My favorite authors never let me down, and I never tire of reading and rereading stories that inspire."

"My reading is much more frivolous," Alice admitted. "I'll take a nice cozy mystery anytime, as you well know."

"Maybe mysteries satisfy you because the line is always drawn between good and evil. They're moral tales for the modern age."

"I hadn't thought of it that way, but I do like everything to be neatly wrapped up at the end. I don't care at all for stories where the criminal gets away."

Viola loved book talk almost as much as she loved books, but Alice had to get back to the inn. She was a permanent substitute nurse at Potterston Hospital, and there was always a possibility that they would need her before her scheduled weekend shift. Even if the hospital didn't need her, Friday was a busy day. There was marketing to do and any number of chores to finish before their new guests began arriving. And, of course, the fawn would need feeding again, and she had to call Jack O'Hara to learn whether he'd found a deer-friendly refuge for her.

Alice finished her tea and took her leave of Viola, promising to keep her posted.

"Oh, I nearly forgot," Viola called after her as she went out the door. "I may have an extra kitten in need of a home, depending on how many are in the litter. Would you like another cat for the inn?"

"Oh, please don't tempt me," Alice said with a broad smile. "You know how hard it is for me to resist furry little creatures."

Jane enjoyed greeting the inn's guests, so she didn't mind in the least that Alice and Louise were busy elsewhere Friday afternoon.

Louise had finished an after-school piano lesson and left to pick up her car at the service station after a tire rotation. Alice had gone to Potterston on some errands after trying unsuccessfully to reach Jack O'Hara. Jane was scrubbing the countertops and reorganizing her small appliances, wondering why no one had ever invented a neater way of cleaning crumbs out of a toaster. No matter how busy she was, she much preferred to take care of her own kitchen. It was her domain, and she liked everything to be just so. It helped immensely in meal preparation if everything was organized her way. Her sisters were both neat with their own things, but only the chef should decide where and how to keep the tools of her trade.

"Hello. Is anyone here?"

Jane was surprised by the call coming from the front hall, where they had a desk to register guests. Although the front door was always unlocked to welcome visitors during the day, she usually heard people arrive before they entered. She hurried toward the entryway and saw a statuesque woman standing beside the largest piece of luggage that had ever passed through the inn's door.

"Ah, there you are," the woman said in a booming but jovial voice. "I'm Ann Baldwin. If you don't mind, I'll leave my suitcase here while I get the rest of my luggage."

"Can I help you?" Jane asked, a little overwhelmed by the larger-than-life woman with long, flowing, gray-blonde curls.

"No need. I've got it all on the front porch. You can hold the door open if you like."

"Glad to," Jane said.

Jane was tall and didn't often look up at another woman, but their new guest towered over her. Even in flat sandals she was well over six feet. She had lively blue eyes in a face with strong features. It was unwrinkled except for pleasant laugh lines at the corners of her eyes. Jane couldn't begin to guess how old she was, but her shoulders were broad and strong looking with no hint of a stoop. In fact, their new guest reminded her of a long-forgotten picture of a warrior-queen's statue in Britain, a heroic figure driving a chariot against the Romans. It was an odd image for Jane to conjure up, but the woman only reinforced it when she brought more luggage into the hallway. She was carrying a second huge suitcase and two smaller cases.

Her clothing certainly reinforced the heroic image. It flowed around her. She was wearing a long skirt made of two layers of filmy material in a floral pattern of pastel blue and purple over royal blue. Her top was made of the same gossamer fabric with purple under lavender and tiny white violets in the design. The hems of both garments were irregular as though cut on the bias so that she seemed to be swaying even when she was standing still.

"One more load," she said cheerfully, depositing the cases beside her first oversized suitcase. "No one can accuse me of traveling light."

Jane held the door as she hoisted a large canvas bag onto one shoulder and wheeled another case over the threshold.

"Maybe I should have held onto Nan's room for my luggage," she said with a laugh. "She said to give you her apologies. She was really sorry to cancel at the last minute, but sometimes family has to come first. Do you have kids?"

"No," Jane said, "but I have a niece, my sister Louise's daughter. She's grown up and on her own."

"My kids are too. I have two daughters, Cindy and Janie. The younger, that's Janie, went to Phoenix to live near her father, my ex, and Cindy is married and living in Kansas City. I'll be going there in August. No grand kiddies yet, but I can hardly wait."

"I'm Jane Howard. Your friend doesn't need to worry about canceling. We have a waiting list, and I've already booked her room for people who wanted shorter stays. If you'll sign in, I'll show you your room."

Jane looked at the mountain of luggage and wished for the first time that they had a bellhop.

"How did you hear about Grace Chapel Inn?" Jane asked as she went through the formalities of registering Ann Baldwin.

"A friend of a friend of Nan's told her about it. If the bedrooms are as cozy as the outside, it was a good tip."

"You're from Kalamazoo. We've never had a guest from there."

"Nan and I are both into antiquing, so she probably heard about you through that network. I think some antiques dealer her friend knows has stayed here."

"It could be the Larsens," Jane said, happy to make the connection. "Do you know them?"

"No, but then, as I said, it was a word-of-mouth thing with my friend Nan. I was in the newspaper game a long time. I know how information—and rumors—can spread."

"Oh, were you a reporter?"

Jane was learning more about this new guest than she knew about some of their neighbors. She wasn't surprised to learn that Ann Baldwin was a professional communicator.

"A lifestyle writer. Now I just freelance. I like the freedom of working when I feel like it and doing projects of my own."

She shifted the huge needlepoint bag on her shoulder that served as her purse and replaced the credit card that Jane had used to check her in.

"Of course, I'd better feel like it often enough to pay the bills," Ann said with one of her startlingly vigorous laughs.

"The guest rooms are on the second floor," Jane said, almost apologizing for the trip up the stairs with all that luggage. "I'll help you carry your cases."

"If you'll just take my slide projector and that other bag, I'll handle the rest."

Jane was curious about the luggage, but she didn't want to ask about it. She already felt a bit nosy for knowing so much about a guest who'd just arrived.

"That's why I picked Acorn Hill," Ann said without any prompting. "It's midway between two towns where I'm giving talks. It's a long way to travel for my church presentations, but I'm here for a vacation too."

"Our family is active in our church. My father was the minister of Grace Chapel. You probably saw it on your way here."

"A pretty little church just down the road?" Ann hoisted a big case in either hand and started following Jane toward the stairs.

"Yes, that's it. Do you mind if I ask what your presentation is?"

"I'd be disappointed if you didn't," she said with a chuckle. "I'm the postcard lady."

Jane drew a blank on that, so she said nothing.

"I hold mail auctions to sell collectible postcards. All the proceeds go to our church's hunger-relief program. It's been written up in a couple of church publications, so I get donations from other churches across the country. I even got some once from a missionary in Senegal. Occasionally, a church wants to know how the sales work. Usually the women's guilds are the ones who are interested. It just so happens that I received invitations to speak from two in this area. I love Pennsylvania in May, so here I am. I'm just sorry my friend has to miss it."

"It sounds like a really interesting project," Jane said. She liked people with the initiative to do unusual things, and their new guest certainly seemed to be full of ideas. A project to help feed hungry people especially appealed to her.

"Perhaps you'd like to hear more about my postcard project later on?"

"Yes, indeed. I'll look forward to learning more."

The stairs didn't seem to slow Ann in the least. She didn't even plunk her cases down when they reached the second floor and Jane opened the door of the guest room for her.

"You have the Sunset Room, so you have a private bath," Jane explained as she let Ann go ahead of her into one of the rooms she'd decorated after she and her sisters had decided to turn the family home into a bed-and-breakfast.

"Pretty," Ann said as she deposited her cases beside a creamy antiqued dresser that stood out against terra-cotta walls hung with impressionist prints. "Ah, a Renoir. His colors are so appealing that I want to absorb them into myself."

"I've never thought of it quite that way, but I know how you feel," Jane said. "If I could paint one square inch the way he did, I would consider myself a real artist."

Jane surprised herself by acknowledging this to a stranger, but something about the new guest drew confidences. Maybe it was because Ann was completely open about herself. Jane felt that she knew her already, although she'd only been there for a few minutes.

"Perhaps I can help you with these items," Jane quickly offered.

"I won't hear of it. If a woman loads herself down with a truckload of baggage, she should be ready to be her own mule."

"But it's no trouble."

"I've been sitting in that car since dawn. If anybody needs a little exercise, it's me. Besides, having my post-card equipment in my room will allow me to prepare my presentation."

Jane couldn't help smiling as she returned to the kitchen. Sometimes running a bed-and-breakfast was more fun than a circus.

Chapter Seven

*L*ouise began her Saturday by reading from her Bible. She couldn't count the times a randomly selected verse had given her guidance throughout the day. So often when things were stressful, she would recall the words she had read that morning and be comforted by them.

Dawn had arrived with clear skies and the promise of a perfect May day. Louise felt full of gratitude for the richness of her life and the love that filled it; all was well with her. And yet, a nagging doubt invaded her thoughts from time to time: Was it appropriate for her to try to teach Diana how to drive? Her own daughter had learned quickly and easily with a little coaching from her father, so Louise had absolutely no experience as a driving instructor. It was only Lara Zale's urgent plea for help that made her even consider it.

The Scriptures didn't seem to offer an answer to her dilemma—at first. Then she read through some favorite passages in the New Testament and focused on the account of Jesus calling his disciples Peter and Andrew. "At once they left their nets and followed him" (Matthew 4:20).

The same happened as James and John, the sons of Zebedee, were helping their father with his fishing net. They left their father and the boat and immediately followed Jesus. They had no idea of what they were called to do. They acted on faith alone, and often Christ's followers were still asked to do just that.

Louise closed her Bible and felt reassured. Maybe Diana wasn't meant to be a driver; maybe she was. But Louise would do her best to teach the girl and to trust the Lord. She'd always been a safe driver herself. Maybe she was chosen to instill good road sense into her pupil, lessons that could save lives sometime in the future.

Louise came down from her third-floor bedroom, trying not to let the stairs creak as she went. The inn was quiet with no telltale sounds from the guest rooms on the second floor. Every room was occupied, which meant Jane was probably hard at work preparing breakfast. Moments later Louise reached the bottom of the stairs and detected an appetizing aroma.

She'd given Diana an early time to have their first lesson. They would start on the roads in Acorn Hill Park, and Louise wanted to finish before people flocked there to enjoy the pleasant day. Fortunately, the park had scenic trails for early morning walkers and runners, so they would have the roadway to themselves. It was too soon to think of a location for the second and third lessons.

"Good morning," Louise said as she walked into the kitchen.

"Full house," Jane said, too wrapped up in her preparations for small talk. "I've been wanting to use my ramekins, so I'm making baked eggs Lorraine."

Louise watched for a moment while Jane arranged a gleaming sheet of waxed paper on the counter, then skillfully used a cheese slicer to produce almost paper-thin slices of Gruyère.

"I'll just get myself some cereal," Louise offered. "You have a big group to feed."

"You'll do no such thing," her younger sister scolded. "I'm counting on you to taste test. I've already minced the bacon, so it won't take long to bake your egg in a water bath."

"It's a lot of work just for me," Louise said, then realized that Jane was giving her a stern look. "I know, you love cooking. I keep equating it with work because for me, it is."

Jane put a fresh fruit cup in front of her at the table and proudly announced that it was *Macédoine de fruits*. Louise quickly decided that the serving of fresh pineapple, strawberries and peaches, probably the ones Jane had frozen herself last year, deserved a fancy name. She detected traces of ginger and lemon in the blend and found the treat to be wonderful.

While Louise savored every bite, Jane heated a small amount of cream and assembled the egg, cheese, bacon bits and seasoning in a ramekin.

"You need a good breakfast if you're going to give a good driving lesson," Jane said as she set the cup to bake in a water bath.

"I'm trying to be optimistic about the three lessons," Louise said. "If all goes well, I may do more, but at least I'll be giving Diana a fair trial."

"You have a choice of baked goods," Jane said, focused on food preparation as she was whenever she cooked. "I'm baking cinnamon twists, and I have a *kugelhopf*, my raisin-almond coffee cake, ready to cut. Or I can give you a slice of honey-bran bread."

"Have you done all that this morning?" Louise asked, a bit floored by Jane's output even though she was entirely familiar with her sister's energy in the kitchen.

"No," Jane said with a soft laugh. "The honey-bran bread was in the freezer. I had the unbaked twists there too. I made the coffeecake yesterday because it heats up nicely. And the *Macédoine de fruits* had to sit for a while, so I made it up last night."

"I wish I had as good a handle on my job of teaching Diana to drive," Louise said wistfully. "She's had so many lessons already, I don't know what to expect."

"She's a good piano student, isn't she?" Jane asked.

"Yes, but when she puts her foot on a piano pedal, it doesn't streak across the room and hit a tree," Louise said, losing the battle against dread. She almost envied Alice, whose worst job of the day would be cleaning up after the fawn—unless she pulled emergency-room duty on her shift.

"I wonder how our orphan is doing this morning," she said. It wasn't helping in the least to dwell on the lesson.

"I haven't checked yet. I think Alice likes to take care of her herself. She's done all the feeding so far, and it seems to be going well. She finally reached Jack yesterday, and he is still trying to locate a more suitable place for our little friend."

Louise chose a toasted slice of the honey-bran bread to go with her egg dish, and her breakfast allowed her to forget her driving challenge for a while. After she cleared her dishes, thanked Jane and complimented her on her delicious cooking, she went upstairs to prepare for her eight o'clock meeting with Diana. It was early to expect a teen to be up and ready for a lesson on the weekend, but avoiding other traffic was Louise's first priority. There was nothing she could do about natural hazards like trees, ditches and big rocks.

She drove to Diana's house and parked her car on the street. They would use the Zales' second car for the lessons, because her father had bought it for his daughter's use. Diana had been watching for her and came out on the front porch before Louise got out of her car.

This morning Diana looked especially young. She'd pulled her hair back into two bobbing tails on either side of her head, and the top she was wearing with her jeans had layers of pink ruffles that reminded Louise of a little girl's Sunday school frock. At least she was wearing running shoes that tied, not flip-flops or some other footwear unsuitable for driving. What she didn't have was a purse.

"Hi, Mrs. Smith. I'm all ready to drive." She bounced down the steps and ran up to Louise with car keys dangling from her fingers.

"Good morning, Diana. I'm glad you're ready to go, but haven't you forgotten something?"

Diana gave her the blank stare that teenagers reserve for adults who aren't talking their language.

"Your learner's permit," Louise prompted.

"Oh yeah, I'm supposed to have that with me, aren't I? I'll run back and get it."

Louise sighed as she waited for her return. Louise hoped it was just initial nervousness with a new driving instructor that had made her forget.

Diana opened the garage door and joined Louise in the driveway. "Where do you want me to drive?" she asked, waving the permit to show Louise that she had it.

"I think it would be best if we start with some basics in the park. I'll drive your car there. Then you can take over."

"I can drive there," Diana assured her.

"I'm sure you can, but I need a bit of practice with your car. Mine is much older, and I need to see how yours is different."

"Oh, okay," her pupil said agreeably. "It's not a stick shift or anything tricky."

"I'm sure it's not, but I need to see how it handles."

Diana led her into the garage where a blue hatchback compact was parked. Louise quickly saw that it was much like the one Jane drove, and she didn't expect any problems driving it herself. She got into the car, and Diana joined her in the front seat.

"Suppose you tell me what to do now," Louise said, hitting on that strategy to see if Diana had mastered the basics.

"Just start the engine and back out," she said.

"We're not quite ready for that."

"Oh yeah, gotta put on the seat belts." She fastened her own and waited for Louise to do the same.

"I'm sure your other teachers have told you to use them, but I can't emphasize enough how important they are."

"I hope you're not going to tell me about a bunch of accidents where people got killed not wearing them.

It makes me nervous to hear everything that could go wrong."

Already this wasn't going well.

"Now what should I do?" Louise asked as patiently as she could.

"Back out."

"One of your brothers could be skateboarding in the driveway."

"They're still sleeping."

"Diana, we're going to waste a lot of time if you don't give this your full attention. What must I do before backing up?"

The pupil looked contrite. "You check behind you," she said.

"How?"

"Rearview mirror, side mirrors, rear window. I passed all the rules on my written test, Mrs. Smith. I just need a little practice driving."

"Before you get behind the wheel, I have to be convinced that you know the rules."

"Do I have to start at the beginning again?"

Instead of responding, Louise backed out the car and started toward the park.

"I'm sorry for being impatient," Diana said after a minute of silence. "It's just that I know how to drive. I just get rattled when I have to take a road test. It's so unfair that I can't get a passing mark."

"Let's see if we can figure out why that is," Louise said in a kind voice. "Give it your full concentration, and we'll see what needs to be improved."

"Okay," her pupil agreed. "But I don't think the man at the license bureau likes female drivers. I bet if I were a boy, I would've passed."

"I hope that's not true," Louise said. The last thing she wanted was a debate about the integrity of the driving inspector. "Did he tell you what areas you need to work on?"

"He checked a whole bunch: lane changing, failure to yield right of way, braking, left turns, parallel parking. No one has to parallel park anymore. The mall has drive-in spaces. I don't see why that was on the test."

"We'll practice it anyway," Louise said, trying to ignore the sinking feeling in her stomach. What had she gotten herself into?

The compact handled well, although Louise noticed that she had to step on the brake harder than she did on her old Cadillac, and, of course, that there wasn't as much power in Diana's car. The park was nearly deserted as Louise pulled to a stop. They saw a runner off in the distance, and an older couple was walking on one of the footpaths, but they had the roadway to themselves. Louise knew she had to relinquish the steering wheel to her pupil. She turned off the engine, murmured a little prayer under her breath and hoped for the best.

Diana slid behind the wheel while Louise got into the passenger seat. Perhaps she was worrying too much. Her pupil put on her seat belt, adjusted the mirrors, started the car and eased away from the shoulder, checking first to be sure nothing was coming even though they hadn't seen any other cars in the park.

"Nicely done," Louise said, suspecting that Diana needed confidence as much as she needed practice.

"How fast should I go?" she asked.

"Have you seen a speed sign?"

"Not really," her pupil weakly admitted.

"When you've had more driving experience, you'll automatically notice road signs. There's a fifteen-mile-per-hour limit within the park. Do you know why?"

"Too many people walking around?" Diana guessed.

"Especially children who might take a shortcut from one play area to another."

Diana began to circle the park at exactly fifteen miles per hour, and Louise relaxed a bit for the first time since getting into the car with her. If all she needed was practice, the lessons might not be too trying.

Suddenly Diana slammed hard on the brakes, catching Louise unprepared. Even at that speed, her body strained against the seat belt, and she had an instant of panic.

"Why did you stop?" Louise didn't see anything in the road that required an abrupt stop. In fact, the way ahead was deserted.

"I didn't want to hit that bird."

"A bird?"

"It flew away, but I was afraid of hitting it."

Louise could feel her heart pounding, and it took her a moment to decide how to handle Diana's braking technique.

"I would hate to hit any kind of animal," Louise admitted, "but birds are really fast. You're very unlikely to hit one, especially not at town speeds. If a car had been behind you, you could have been rear-ended."

"There wasn't."

"Did you know that from looking in your rearview mirror, or did you just assume?"

"Mrs. Smith, there's almost no one in the park at this time of day," she said.

"You're right, but let's pretend this is a street in town. You have to look out for all the usual hazards."

Louise could see where she'd made her first mistake as a driving instructor. She should have quizzed Diana's mother about the reasons for her daughter's failing the driving test. She had a sinking feeling that she would soon learn the reasons on her own.

To Diana's credit, she did have the responsibility to avoid wildlife if possible, but she would have to learn not to do so at the risk of human lives. Louise wasn't completely sure how she would've reacted if the fawn's mother had run in front of her car. From everything she'd heard about deer accidents, the driver seldom had time to make a decision.

Louise couldn't think about that now. She had to concentrate fully on what Diana was doing. Glancing out the window on her side of the car, she was surprised to see Mr. Horton, an elderly resident of Acorn Hill, passing them on his bicycle. He waved at Louise as he passed, and it wasn't hard to see that he was smirking, as well he might. The old fellow probably didn't pass cars very often.

Diana was barely moving at five miles per hour.

"You can go a little faster," Louise prompted.

"What if a squirrel or something runs in front of me?"

Was Diana really worried about hitting something, or did she just feel safer driving at a crawl? Working with teenagers was a tricky proposition. They could be wildly enthusiastic one day and uncooperative the next, giving few clues to the reasons for their behavior.

"Just watch out for the man on the bike," she said, sneaking a peek at her wristwatch. They'd agreed to an hour of driving. Louise decided to calculate the time from their starting point at the Zale house. She doubted her pupil would protest.

"I don't know how to pass bikes," Diana said. "Can't I wait until he gets out of the way?"

"Oh dear," Louise said under her breath. "Well, why don't you pull over, and we'll practice backing up?"

"That's my worst thing."

"All the more reason to practice."

"Oh, okay." She crept to the side and stopped with one side of the car on the grass and the other on the asphalt.

"That's fine."

"What should I do now?" Every word expressed her hesitation about doing anything with the car. Louise had to wonder whether learning to drive was mostly her mother's idea. Diana showed none of the eagerness to learn that made her an excellent piano student.

"See that tree about fifty yards back? Put the car in reverse and see if you can back up so you'll be alongside it."

"Oh dear." Diana sounded genuinely distressed by the challenge. "That tree is pretty close to the road. My dad will really be upset if I hit another tree."

"Another?" Louise didn't press it. She didn't want to know. "It's a good ten feet from the road. You are not going to hit it. I'll watch out the back window and warn you if you come anywhere close."

"Well, okay."

Diana backed the car cautiously, making jerky stops every few yards.

"Straighten the wheel! You're turning it too much!" Louise watched with alarm as Diana headed directly toward one of the stately maples that made the park such a delight. "Stop!"

"See, I told you backing up is my worst thing."

"Go forward, then try again. It takes a little practice to get the knack of going in reverse."

On the fourth try, Louise decided that it was going to take a miracle.

"Let's just concentrate on going forward for the rest of the lesson," she said, checking first to be sure Mr. Horton was safely out of range.

Diana made a circuit of the park without incident, at one point even getting the car's speed up to fifteen miles per hour. Louise had her repeat it two more times until Diana protested.

"It's really boring, just driving around the park. Can I drive home now?"

Could she? If Louise said no, would it shatter her fragile confidence? If she said yes, would they arrive safe and sound? She thought of all the potential hazards on the way and reluctantly decided that she needed to show confidence in Diana. After all, she must have done a lot of street driving with her other teachers. Of course, they no doubt had a second brake as a safely precaution. Louise edged her left foot a little closer to the pedals, hoping her pupil didn't notice.

"Yes. Drive home." Louise prayed that they would get there safely and angled her upper body to be as close to the steering wheel as possible.

Diana's face was scrunched up in concentration as she headed toward the park exit. The stop sign loomed ahead just as she started to accelerate. Louise opened her mouth to warn Diana, but it was too late. She drove past the traffic sign as though it didn't exist.

Louise gasped and instinctively slammed her foot on the floorboard, but it was a futile gesture. Only Diana could reach the brake pedal. She pulled out onto the street in the middle of two lanes, but fortunately no cars were in sight.

Knees trembling, Louise watched helplessly as Diana moved on, gradually getting up to twenty miles per hour. There were no stoplights between the park and her home, and she managed to get to her subdivision without straying into the oncoming lane, although Louise had an anxious moment when Diana let the car wander onto the shoulder, then speeded up, plowing a furrow of dirt and gravel.

A few blocks from her house, she stopped in the middle of the road.

"Maybe you'd better drive from here," Diana said.

"You're nearly home."

"Yes, but my brothers will be out on their skateboards."

"I'm sure they'll get out of your way."

"Oh, you don't know my brothers. They'll skate around the car just to tease me. They think it's a big joke that I flunked my driving test."

"Tell you what. Just drive up behind my car and park on the street. They won't have a chance to bother you."

Louise had a bad moment as Diana pulled to within inches of her back bumper before coming to a stop, but the lesson was over. She could breathe easily again.

Diana was right about her brothers being out on their skateboards, but they kept their distance, more intent on their activity than their sister. Louise got out of the car and smiled as the pair of freckled towheads streaked toward their house.

"If those are your brothers, they're good on their skateboards," Louise said, watching as they slid around the driveway.

"Jeremy and Josh, this is Mrs. Smith." Diana called out, pointing first at the taller one in a black T-shirt with a fluorescent green logo, then at the smaller one, who was grinning at his sister.

"Are you boys into any other sports?" Louise asked.

They stood still for a minute to tell her they liked soccer and hockey.

"It will be nice when Diana can drive you to practices, won't it?"

"If she ever gets her license," the older boy said skeptically.

"Of course she'll get it," Louise said, hoping she sounded confident.

"Yeah, like that's going to happen in this century," Jeremy said.

"Or the next." Josh laughed at his own humor.

"I'm sure pretty soon she'll be driving you to practices and games." Louise was trying to convince Diana, not her brothers.

"We have friends who will pick us up," Jeremy declared.

"Yes, I imagine you do. But sometimes friends' parents are too busy. You can depend on Diana when she passes her driving test."

"If she passes," Jeremy said. He sounded less than certain about her competence.

"Of course she will. I've given hundreds and hundreds of lessons, and I know Diana is a good student. She just needs practice."

She smiled faintly as she left the Zale children. It wasn't her style to lie to anyone, much less children, but technically, she hadn't. She'd just omitted mentioning that all the lessons she'd given had been on the piano. Diana had enough trouble driving without her mischievous brothers doubting her.

$\backsim$

Alice was glad that she was in the kitchen helping Jane wash the dishes when Jack O'Hara stopped by. He was out of uniform but was quick to announce his reason for being there.

"I got a complaint about a stray dog wandering around Acorn Hill. You know I'm technically on duty 24–7. Calls come to my cell phone no matter where I am or what I'm doing."

"We don't have many loose dogs in town," Alice said. "I rarely see one that isn't on a chain or leash when I'm out walking."

"Well, there's no reason to be alarmed. It sounds like a young Lab that got loose by mistake. Probably not danger-ous, but I thought you'd want to know in case it comes around your shed. I'll leave my cell number in case you see it. How's the fawn doing, by the way?"

"She's started feeding, although we have to use a rubber glove. She still won't take a baby nipple. But she's standing up," Alice reported.

"I wasn't at all sure she would survive the first night," Jack admitted. "Poor little thing was terrified. Reminded me of the *Bambi* movie. Bet I've watched it twenty times on DVD. My boys loved it when they were little. Truth to tell, I still do."

"I hope our fawn story has a happy ending," Alice said in a worried tone.

"Have you gotten any leads on where we can take it?" Jane asked as she put a cup of coffee and a plate of freshly baked and frosted carrot cookies in front of the ever-appreciative Jack.

"Not so far, I'm afraid. I've been asking around in hopes of getting a lead. If there's a place in this county, I'll find it eventually. I know the fawn can't stay in your shed much longer."

"I hope it's soon," Alice said. "Not that I wouldn't keep the fawn permanently if it were possible, but I feel for it, cooped up in our gardening shed."

"That's probably the best thing about the *Bambi* film. The animals got along without human intervention. Man was the enemy. That part was true to life. But now that we've taken responsibility for a fawn, you can be sure I'll stay on the case."

"We really appreciate that," Jane said.

"Raising a fawn is even more complicated than I realized," Alice said. "I'm going to need more straw for bedding and I'll have to keep an eye on the formula."

They heard the front door slam shut and looked up as Louise walked into the kitchen.

"I need tea, lots of tea."

Alice stared with surprise at her usually immaculate sister. Louise's short silver hair looked somewhat disheveled. She was wearing a practical khaki skirt that had somehow slipped around so the side zipper was halfway to the front. Her butter-yellow oxford cloth shirt had one sleeve rolled up and one down.

"Oh, hello, Jack. Have you come to take the fawn to a better location?" Louise asked.

"Afraid not," Jack said, obviously not quite sure how to react to a flustered, disheveled Louise.

"How did the driving lesson go?" Jane ventured to ask.

"She brakes for birds."

Chapter Eight

*A*lice always enjoyed it when the young members of the congregation had the opportunity to plan a Sunday service at Grace Chapel, so she expected an interesting experience as she walked to church with her sisters. Several of the young girls involved in planning it were ANGELs, members of the group she had founded and still led. The girls involved in it now were especially lively and imaginative, so there could be some surprises in store.

"I wonder what the kids will come up with," Jane said as the three of them walked to the chapel together.

She wore her dark hair pulled back in a bun, and Alice thought she looked sophisticated in her turquoise suit with a white silk blouse. She was so thankful her younger sister had decided to join them in running their bed-and-breakfast. Working together had given the three of them a special closeness that went beyond growing up together.

"Nothing that will shock our elderly members, I hope," Louise said. It was difficult to tell if she was being serious.

Alice always thought of her older sister as unflappable. She looked like her usual self this morning in a pretty blue dress with a narrow belt and white collar, but within she was still uneasy about giving driving instructions.

"No doubt Rev. Thompson has creative control," Jane said. "He probably had them rehearse the whole service."

"Yes, I'm sure we can trust Kenneth to give them guidance," Alice said.

"I guess." Usually Louise was one of their minister's strongest supporters, but she didn't seem confident about anything this morning.

"We have so many talented young musicians in the congregation," Alice said, still trying to cheer up her sister. "It's a treat to have them doing all the music this morning."

They reached the front door of the chapel, and Jane went off to chat with a friend before going inside. Louise led the way to their usual pew, and Alice joined her in prayer and contemplation before the service began.

The young people followed the usual order of the service, but they had selected their own music. Alice was thoroughly enjoying it and was especially pleased when one of her ANGELs gave a homily. Emily had a vibrant voice that faltered a bit at first but grew more confident as she went on. She began by reading a verse from one of Alice's favorite hymns:

All things bright and beautiful,
All creatures great and small,
All things wise and wonderful,
The Lord God made them all.

An Irish woman, Cecil Frances Alexander, wrote it many years ago as a hymn for children. Alice, however, thought it spoke to all ages and all times.

Emily's message was a simple one, but she spoke with eloquence once she was over her initial nervousness. She reminded the congregation that God had given His people a wonderful world and all that was in it. Everyone who loved God had a special responsibility to cherish and care for all His great gifts.

Alice was genuinely touched. She glanced over at Louise and Jane and was pleased to see warm smiles on their faces too.

"That was a lovely service," Louise said when they went outside to greet friends. "I guess the young have something to teach us if we have the wisdom to listen. It helped me make a decision. I won't give up on Diana's driving yet. I need to find out why she makes so many mistakes when she's driving compared to so few when she's playing the piano. It's almost like dealing with two different girls."

"I'm sure you'll figure it out," Jane said. "Oh, there's one of our guests. I didn't know Ann Baldwin was coming to the service. I'll go say hello and see whether she wants to walk back with us."

Jane walked over to their statuesque guest. This morning Ann wore a fringed velvet shawl that hung down in back over the top of an ankle-length periwinkle blue skirt. The shawl was a blend of gold and orange with traces of blues and greens and reminded Jane of an antique piano cover. Given Ann's interest in antiques, she could very well be wearing just that. Jane had to appreciate their guest's flamboyant style.

Several women of the congregation were admiring the shawl, while Jane admired Ann's ability to make herself part of any group. Earlier she had kept the other inn guests laughing and talking long after they'd finished their breakfast of pecan pancakes and country sausage.

"I didn't know you were coming to church this morning," Jane said when the other women had moved on.

"I was looking for the girl who gave the talk. I want to tell her what a nice job she did."

"She left with her parents, but I'll tell her for you next time I see her. Would you like to walk back to the inn with us?"

Jane looked around for her sisters but didn't see them. They must have headed back without her.

"I guess that would be with *me*. They seem to have gone ahead."

"Don't mind if I do," Ann said. "It's really convenient that you live so close to church, and your inn is one of the nicest I've come across. It must work out well, three sisters running a business together."

"Thank you. I guess you could call it a labor of love," Jane said as they headed toward the inn. "We've learned and experienced so much in the short time Grace Chapel Inn has been open. How is your vacation shaping up? Have you found some good places for antiquing?"

"I've been studying the *Antique Trader*. They put out a regional guide from time to time as well as a weekly calendar of events. I'm overwhelmed with choices."

"It's wonderful weather for antiquing," Jane said a bit wistfully, inhaling air made fragrant by the many nearby bushes in bloom.

"I can't decide whether to head for a big show or flea market or just drive along back roads. Either way, finding anything is a matter of luck. I don't want to spend all my time driving, but I'm more likely to find bargains in out-of-the-way places. At least that's my theory," she said with a hearty laugh. "It's a shame my friend had to cancel. Two are a lot more fun than one. Say, would you like to join me?"

"I'd love to, but I have a lot to do at the inn. Our busy season is beginning," Jane said.

"Except for the two talks I have to give, I'm flexible. Name a day when you can get away, and we'll hit the road together."

"I'm tempted. It sounds like fun. Why don't I check my calendar and talk to my sisters. If Alice is free to cover for me, there's no reason why I can't take a day off once breakfast is over."

"You can bet I won't be missing any of your breakfasts. Today's was out of this world, but don't worry. I won't ask for your secret recipe. When it comes to cooking, I'm a great guest."

Jane laughed, excited at the prospect of antiquing with such a pleasant person. She knew Louise and Alice would urge her to take a day off.

"We'll work out a time," she promised.

When they got back to the inn, Ann hurried up to her room to get ready for her day of antiquing. Jane heard voices in the kitchen, so she joined her sisters there before going up to change out of her good clothes. She could tell by the tone of their voices that something was wrong.

"At least she didn't injure herself," Louise was saying in a soothing tone.

"Not that I could see," Alice said, "but who knows what will happen if she keeps getting more frisky."

"What's up?" Jane was pretty sure it was a fawn problem; she listened as Alice related her latest worry.

"When I went to check, I could tell right away that the poor thing had been trying to get out. The straw was trampled and strewn everywhere, and the water dish was overturned. The lantern I'd left on the worktable was tipped over. She must have been banging against the supports for that to happen. I didn't go inside for fear of panicking her, but I felt like a prison guard. You don't know how badly I wished I could leave the door open and let the sweet creature go."

Jane shook her head sadly. She knew exactly how Alice felt.

Wendell rubbed against Jane's ankles, his tactful way of reminding her that he hadn't had his morning treat. She smiled and obliged, taking one of his favorite tidbits from the supply she kept for him.

"There's nothing like a fawn in the shed to make me appreciate our self-sufficient tabby," she said affectionately as she handed over the treat.

"We obviously need to move the fawn soon," Louise said.

"If anyone can find a better temporary home, Jack can. I know he's trying hard," Jane said, trying to hold out some hope for a solution.

"You're probably right," Louise agreed.

"There's something I wanted to talk to both of you about," Jane said. "Ann Baldwin has asked me to go antiquing with her. I'm a little hesitant to leave for a whole day because we're booked solid for the next few weeks."

"There's not a reason in the world why you shouldn't go," Alice said. "Everyone needs a day off. You should have insisted that you have more time to yourself. You work too hard."

"I never think of cooking as work. I love being a part of our own business. As for time off, I'll only go at a time when both of you can be here without rearranging your schedules," she insisted.

"I'm not on call Tuesday," Alice said.

"Tuesday is fine with me. I don't have any lessons until school is out, which means I can cover most of the day," Louise said.

"Tuesday it is then." Jane felt a rush of pleasure at the thought of spending a day with Ann. "We won't leave until after breakfast, so you don't need to worry about cooking."

She felt a little guilty for feeling so happy at the same time that Alice was stressed about the fawn and Louise was dreading the next driving lesson. It seemed like a good time to change the subject.

"The youngsters really did a nice job today. Emily's homily was lovely," she said.

"It did make me feel we've done the right thing about the fawn," Alice said. "She is one of God's creatures."

"I was nearly ready to back out of the driving lessons," Louise admitted. "Emily reminded me of what young people can accomplish when they're moved by faith. What I need to do is figure out why a good piano student like Diana can't master the rules and techniques of driving."

"I think the piano is much, much harder than a car, but then I'm tone-deaf," Jane said.

"Do you have any clues? That's what we have to do with patients at the hospital. Look for clues that will help the doctors diagnose their problems. Maybe that's why I like reading mysteries so much," Alice said.

"When you put it that way, I do have several clues. Diana was worried about hitting a tree and—"

"You didn't tell us anything about a tree," Jane interrupted.

"She didn't hit one, although the way she backs up, it was a small miracle that she didn't hit several. She seemed very concerned about collisions, even when the prospect of having one was slight. Maybe she's a nervous driver because she can't forget past mistakes. That would help explain why her mother asked me to give lessons. She wants someone who will encourage her, not just instruct her. This is all so new to me. My Eliot was more than willing to give Cynthia some help when she was a beginner, so I've never really taught anyone to drive. He was a born teacher. Not all fathers are so patient, I imagine."

"Maybe Diana's dad tried to help but didn't have as much patience as you do," Alice said. "Of course, that's just a theory. He may be too busy."

"He does travel in his job, so we have to reserve judgment, I guess," Jane said.

"She can't possibly have taken as many lessons as she has without absorbing the basics." Louise was thinking aloud. "But she made mistakes that only a beginner would make. And it's not because she isn't an intelligent girl. I've had proof that she is. She's quick to grasp new concepts in music. She should be able to qualify for a license."

"Unless she's hopeless at driving," Jane said sympathetically. "I'm speaking as someone who cried every time she sat down to practice the piano."

"You only took a few lessons," Louise reminded her.

"It was enough," Alice said emphatically, knowing Jane wasn't sensitive about her lack of musical ability. Her other talents more than compensated.

"Anyway, when we drove up to Diana's house, her two younger brothers mocked her about driving. Maybe a combination of past mistakes and her brothers' teasing has sapped her confidence."

"Or maybe she doesn't have the ability to master a car," Jane said. "I've heard of supersmart people who can't do simple tasks. We humans are a complicated species."

"That's true, but Diana has good motor skills. Her problem could be lack of maturity, I guess." Louise didn't sound convinced. "Be that as it may, I have committed myself to three lessons. One down, two to go. I'll keep my word, but I dread every minute in the car with that girl."

With Jane's help, Alice cleaned the shed and fed the fawn. She no longer trusted the poor thing to be docile, although she finally coaxed it to take a few tentative sips from the baby bottle nipple. It would be much easier to give a good feeding if she could dispense with the rubber glove.

The bale of hay was nearly used up, and the formula was going fast now that the fawn had a better appetite. That was another reason to hope that bottle-feeding would work. It was hard not to waste formula transferring it to the leaky glove.

Jane looked forward to her day off, but fawn care was getting harder and harder. It was going to be a struggle to watch the inn and care for the orphan, especially after school hours when Louise's students started coming for piano lessons.

As for Alice, since bringing the fawn home she had slept poorly; however, her work at the hospital would be light again this coming week. Most nurses were saving their vacation time for the summer months when children and husbands were available, and her main function of late was to substitute for those who took sick days or other time off.

The two sisters were walking back to the house when Louise came out the side entrance with the portable phone in hand.

"Call for you, Alice. It's Mark," she said, handing it over and linking arms with Jane to draw her back to the house.

"Hello, Mark."

"Alice, how is your new guest doing?"

"Not liking the accommodations, I would say. There were signs today that she tried to get out."

"She didn't injure herself, did she?"

"No, not that I can see."

"Is she eating?"

"Yes, but not from a bottle at first. We had to try a method that Aunt Ethel used on the farm to keep lambs and kids alive, feeding from the finger of a rubber glove. It's not a very efficient method."

"I'm sure if anyone can get her to eat, it's you. How is the colostrum holding out?"

"We're all right for a few more days. Is there some place where I can get more?"

"I'll have some delivered to you, but I have to stay in Cleveland another day. I'll get on it as soon as I get back to Philly."

"I would really appreciate it. I don't know how much longer we can keep her in the shed. It must seem a horrible place to a wild creature."

"I wish I knew more about the options in Pennsylvania. I've been doing some research on my laptop. As soon as I get home, I'll make some phone calls and see what I can turn up."

"That would be wonderful. Have you had a good conference?"

Alice stood in the yard listening to Mark's humorous account of his weekend. When the call was over, she felt reluctant to return to the house. The balmy spring weather provided an invitation to remain outside. She wished she could put a leash on the fawn and take her for a walk. None of God's creatures should be confined in a dark shed on a lovely day like this.

Chapter Nine

$\mathcal{A}$lice liked the morning shift in the emergency room, and Monday was no exception. It was a busy time, but they were more likely to see illnesses than accidents so early in the day. It distressed her to see what people did to themselves through carelessness, but this morning all the patients were there through no fault of their own. Midmorning, a weary-looking mother brought in her twin two-year-old boys because one of them was running a high temperature.

"They usually do things together. I hope they don't this time," the mother joked weakly as Alice prepped the sick child for the doctor. "I mostly take them to the pediatrician, but she's booked solid all morning."

"You did right to bring him here," Alice assured her as she read the thermometer.

"Randy, don't touch that!" his mother said as her healthy son started to investigate the waste receptacle. "No, Ricky, you have to sit on the table until the doctor comes. He's going to make you feel better."

"Jazzy go home now," Randy said, turning his attention to the curtain separating examining stations.

As he made a game of crawling under it, his mother tried to coax him to her side. Alice was prepared for just such an emergency. She took one of her hopping frogs out of a lower drawer and showed the two-year-old how to press it down to make it jump. He giggled and said the word that sounded like "jazzy" again.

"It's his favorite word," his mother explained. "It can mean whatever he wants it to at the moment. He's quite a talker for his age. In fact, he does the talking for both of them."

When the sick twin and his boisterous brother left, Alice had a free moment to muse over their names. She wondered how many times their mother had to use them every day. They were identical twins, and it couldn't be easy to keep them straight.

She wondered what name her fawn should have. "Fawn" just wouldn't work. As far as she knew, all fawns were similar in appearance. Perhaps her little orphan needed the distinction of having a name all its own. The talkative twin had made her smile, so she decided to use his favorite word.

"Jazzy." She softly mouthed the word as she went on to the next patient. She wondered if the other rescuers would like the name as well.

Another thing she liked about starting the day early was getting home in the middle of the afternoon. She could accomplish any number of things before dinner, then enjoy a relaxing evening. Not surprisingly, she found Jane at work in the garden when she returned home.

"Did you have a good day?" Jane asked, standing up from the bed she was planting with annuals.

"Pretty good. We're seeing a run of spring fevers, mostly in children. I had a cute pair of twins, only one sick, but the healthy one was a handful. He gave me an idea, though."

She told Jane about her name choice for the fawn and was surprised when her sister didn't seem to like it.

"We don't have to name it," Alice said.

"Oh no, it's not that," Jane assured her. "It's just that she may not be with us much longer, and it seems harder to let go of a creature with a name. Jack talked to Rose and Samuel Bellwood about taking her."

"Oh, they would be ideal. They raise blue-ribbon sheep and know all about taking care of animals. But do they have room on their farm for a fawn?"

"Possibly. Jack left a note with a recommendation for you to call as soon as you can. He said it's not a done deal, but he thinks they can be persuaded, especially since the fawn is a female."

"I'd better call right away."

"Their number is on the pad beside the kitchen phone. Jack said he would take responsibility for getting her to the farm if they agree. Oh, by the way, she fed from the bottle this morning. That should make it easier to persuade them. Unfortunately she also trashed her bedding. She's awfully restless in there, I'm afraid."

"The bottle-feeding is good news," Alice agreed, although she was sorry to have missed it.

She hurried to the kitchen, trying to decide how to approach the Bellwoods. Even though Jazzy badly needed a better home, Alice wanted to be sure it was one where the fawn would be welcome. It was asking a big favor of the Bellwoods, and she didn't want to give the impression that she expected more than they were able to provide.

The number was written on Jane's pad, but she decided to talk to Jack first. He answered his cell phone and sounded glad to hear from her.

"You know what nice people they are," he assured her. "Rose is as sweet as her prize-winning pies, and Sam likes to help out when he can. They have a sheep pen to keep the fawn safe. You can rely on them to feed it and take care of it, but they're busy with their own animals, so you better stress that we will still be looking for a more appropriate home for our deer. You may have to be persuasive. Oh, got to go. I'm still on duty."

Alice much preferred face-to-face contact to using the phone, but this was something that had to be settled right away.

"Hello, Rose," Alice said when a woman answered the phone.

"Jack O'Hara is a persuasive man," Rose said after Alice had talked awhile. "He's such a nice man. Helped us out when we had a problem with a neighbor's dog going after our sheep."

"He said there's a possibility you can take an orphan fawn. We have it in our gardening shed, but it's a poor place to keep such a lovely creature."

"I should say! It's eating for you, is it?"

"Nursing from a bottle." Alice was glad she could say that as of today. "And my veterinarian friend Mark Graves has promised to look into the options. Meanwhile, we desperately need a better temporary home."

"It will be quite a bit of work at first."

Alice could hear some reluctance in Rose's voice.

"Yes, I'm afraid it will," she agreed, "but you're our only hope. I feel like a jailer, keeping a wild creature penned up the way we have to."

"Town's no place for a fawn. I guess you'd better bring her out here. The atmosphere will be better for her, and she'll have more room to move about."

"That's wonderful! I'll call Jack and make the arrangements. When would be a good time for you?"

"We're pretty much always here this time of year. Just come on out when you can."

Alice thanked her for her kindness, feeling as though a weight had been lifted from her shoulders. She called Jack back, and he agreed to transport the fawn that evening as soon as he finished work. Once it was settled, she decided to let Viola know too.

"That is good news," the bookstore owner said. "Do you have any idea what to do with her if she doesn't like her new quarters?"

"No, but I'm hoping Mark will find a solution. He's working on it for us. Meanwhile, it's a tremendous relief to have found a better place than our shed. I named her Jazzy, by the way." She explained why.

"That's a sweet name. I know she has to go, Alice, but it's a bit like losing an adopted child, isn't it?"

"She's so helpless and so delicate. I'd love to have her living in the woods behind the house where we could see her from time to time," Alice said wistfully. "Of course, that can't possibly be, so I'm grateful to Jack and the Bellwoods for a place in the open air."

"Yes, it's very kind of them. Oh, we had our kittens," Viola proudly announced. "They're absolutely adorable.

You should come see them. I do have one left that isn't spoken for."

"Maybe when things settle down around here, I'll take a look at the litter."

Alice didn't feel strong enough to see the baby kittens without being tempted to take one. If it were totally up to her, she would be willing to bring home the whole litter, but the responsibility for caring for them would fall on Jane. Alice was working mostly day shifts, and summer would be her busy time when other nurses took their vacations. It wouldn't be fair to put more work on her sister, especially not when the inn was heavily booked. Louise, too, had her hands full with piano lessons, not to mention the stressful job of teaching Diana Zale to qualify for a license. Alice would rather take on a zoo full of animals than one teenager behind the wheel of a car.

At least Jane was taking a day off tomorrow. All three of them got so busy that often they forgot about time off for enjoyment. Poking around in musty barns and dusty shops wasn't Alice's idea of fun, but her sister loved rummaging for treasures. She often framed her lovely paintings in recycled frames, and she read cookbooks like Alice read mysteries. Antiquing with their interesting guest would be sheer pleasure for Jane.

Louise wasn't a clock watcher. She appreciated students who arrived on time for their lessons, but usually her days flew by so fast that she had to hustle to be ready to greet the first student scheduled for an after-school lesson. Monday was different. She kept such careful track of time that every hour seemed to have double the usual number of minutes. But no matter how slowly the hands on the clock moved, seven o'clock would come, and Diana would have her second driving lesson.

Louise earnestly wished she could take back her promise of three lessons, but she'd given her word. What she had to decide now was where Diana could safely drive. The park was out. On a lovely spring evening in mid-May, there were sure to be people out enjoying Acorn Hill's pretty walking trails and recreation area.

Louise located a long-forgotten county map in her father's desk in the library and sat down to plot a safe route. There were back roads she had rarely seen or had since abandoned, and she finally decided on the old Dixon Highway, little used since modern expressways had been built more than half a century ago. It seemed that a number of turnoffs led nowhere. It wouldn't be good to get Diana lost, and this area of Pennsylvania could be hilly with lots of twists and turns in the roads. She decided to put the map in her purse just in case. Whether Diana liked it or not, Louise was going to drive until they reached a convenient place to switch seats.

Louise arrived at the Zales' house promptly at seven, and Diana wanted to start driving as soon as they switched cars. Louise, however, was firm about staying behind the wheel until they got to the Dixon Highway.

"I'm not sure of the roads in that area, but they should be pretty deserted," Louise explained. "There are no towns of any size along the stretch I have in mind. You need road experience, but we'll start with a quiet route."

"My last driving teacher let me drive to Potterston."

"That's nice," Louise said mildly. "Now let's get started so we can finish your lesson while we still have light."

Diana looked back at the house, where her mother was watching through a front window. Then she buckled her seat belt. Louise drove back through Acorn Hill. It took longer than she'd expected to reach their destination, but finally she was able to stop at a long-abandoned filling station so the teen could switch to the driver's seat.

Her student executed a reasonable return to the road, remembering to look both ways, although they hadn't seen another vehicle in several minutes. The Dixon Highway was just what Louise had expected, a back road that no longer carried much traffic. The paving was riddled with potholes and cracks, but at the speed Diana was driving those weren't a serious problem.

"You're doing fine," she encouraged. "Stay on your side of the road even though nothing is coming."

She prayed that they wouldn't overtake a tractor or other slow-moving rig that would require passing. The road was narrow, and the ditches on the side were deep in some places. As they drove, the hills became steeper, and the road curved and twisted to follow the contours of the land. Louise began to wish that she had checked out the route in person before bringing Diana here.

They came to a straight stretch, and a pickup truck came up behind them at what seemed like a reckless speed. It streaked past them, flustering Diana and giving Louise an anxious moment, especially when one of the young men in the truck stuck his head out the window and shouted something at them. At least Diana stayed in her lane, not panicking. Louise felt shaky just remembering the way the youngster had breezed through a stop sign during the last lesson. If Diana lost her concentration, there could be nasty consequences.

No sooner had Louise thought of that stop sign than another one appeared at an intersection ahead of them. Her instinct was to call out a warning, but Diana had to learn to watch for signs herself.

Instead of slowing, Diana accelerated, and Louise's heart pounded as she opened her mouth to call out. Then, as suddenly as she'd sped up, she slammed on the brake, stopping only a few feet beyond the sign.

Louise was speechless. She took a great gasp of air, wondering why a girl who could read intricate musical notes on paper couldn't time a road stop.

"You know," Louise said thoughtfully after a long interval, "a stop sign isn't so different from a musical pause. It's all a matter of reading the roadway as you would a line of music. You do that exceptionally well."

"I've never thought of it that way," Diana said. "Things just seem to come up so fast when I'm driving."

"Is it possible that your mind is somewhere else?" She tried to keep her voice gentle.

Diana didn't respond, but she did stay in her lane and keep the car's speed at a steady thirty-five.

"You did very well the last few miles," Louise complimented her after some relatively uneventful minutes. "I think we should turn back as soon as we see a good place."

"How am I going to turn around?" Diana asked, sounding a bit desperate.

"We'll find a place. If you see a side road, turn down it."

They drove farther than Louise might have wished, but finally she saw an opportunity. It was only a dirt road, but it was on the right and would be an easy turn for Diana.

"There, turn there."

Diana slowed to a crawl, then stopped before inching around the corner. Louise wanted to mention the turn signal and the danger of coming to a complete stop before turning off a highway, but she decided not to bring it up until later.

"If there's a road, it should mean people live on it. When we come to a driveway, you can pull in a little ways and back out." Louise checked alongside the road and wasn't happy with the deep ditches that ran along either side.

"I'm not good at backing out."

Louise tried to ignore the panic in her student's voice. After all, if bad came to worse, she could take over the wheel.

"There's a dirt track on your left that leads to a house and some outbuildings. They're so far from the road that you won't need to go anywhere near them. Just turn in a little way, then back up just as if you were leaving your own driveway at home."

Diana stopped just before she got to the dirt track.

"Now turn."

She inched her way into the drive.

"I forget which way to turn the wheel when I back up."

It was so automatic to Louise that she had to think a moment in order to give clear instructions. She opened her mouth to speak, but an outburst of furious barking at the top of the drive gave her pause.

"Dogs!" Diana cried out. "I can't back out. I'll hit them!"

Louise saw at least four large, overly zealous mutts streaking out from the distant buildings to guard their turf.

"Back up now," she ordered.

"I can't."

"You have to. Now, before they get behind the car."

Diana hit the gas and the car jerked forward.

"Reverse it." Louise struggled to sound calmer than she was.

Maybe she should take over, but she wasn't eager to risk leaving the confines of the car. The leader of the dog pack reached their front bumper.

"Now!"

Diana inched backward, but instead of turning to return the way they'd come, she was starting to go in the wrong direction. Louise reluctantly put her hand on the wheel to steer in the right direction.

She took a deep breath, but they weren't through with the dogs. The furious canines weren't ready to give up their prey, and alarming growls came from both sides of the car.

"I'll hit them!" Diana cried out, close to tears.

"No, they're smart enough to keep out of the way. They're just giving you a sendoff." Louise prayed she was right. "Drive just a little faster."

The dogs gave up the chase when the car got back to the Dixon Highway. Louise was glad she hadn't met the people who owned the beasts. With a pack like that guarding their property, it didn't seem likely that they would be the welcoming sort. Diana stopped, and Louise sighed with relief, then said, "We can turn right here." Instead of turning left to return home, Diana turned right.

"No! I meant turn left right here."

"What?" Diana was confused as well as nervous.

"Never mind, dear. That was my fault. Just keep going straight awhile."

This was going to be a longer lesson than Louise had planned for. She only hoped they could get home before dark. If Diana had this much trouble in daylight, what would happen when it became more difficult to see?

"I can't turn around again. I just can't. You'll have to drive." Diana's voice was weak and teary.

"There's no place to stop here. The car is your responsibility." Louise didn't mean to sound harsh, but she wouldn't be doing Diana a favor by bailing her out, even if that was possible at this point.

"I don't know where we're going. I don't have a good sense of direction," her pupil protested.

"I have a map. Maybe there's another way to get back to Acorn Hill."

Louise didn't like reading in the car, but she held the map close to her face and studied the wavy lines that represented roads.

"It doesn't look like you'll have any problems," she said without confidence. "About a quarter inch ahead, there's an intersection. If you turn right—be sure it's right—you'll come to the little town of Mohawk. I haven't been there in ages, but the map shows a road that meanders back to Acorn Hill. It's a little longer to go that way instead of the way we came, but you won't have to turn around again."

"How long is a quarter inch?"

"Just drive, Diana. It won't be far."

There was a reason why Louise had rarely been to Mohawk. The town consisted of a gas station that also sold groceries, a tavern, a church and a scattering of weather-beaten homes planted on the hillside. It seemed to exist only because of a limestone quarry they'd passed a mile or so back. The sun was getting low behind the hills, and Louise very much wanted to drive herself. But if she took over the wheel, what would that do to Diana's confidence?

Louise wasn't a fan of roller coasters, and she hadn't expected to be on one so close to home. The steep road twisted and turned, seemingly taking ten miles to cover one as the crow flies. At least Diana drove so slowly that motion sickness wasn't a problem, but Louise's eyes felt strained from watching the road ahead and on both sides. Her pupil did better when Louise kept quiet, but the teacher in her wanted to scream instructions. There was no centerline, and the car kept straying into the middle of the road, especially as dusk overtook them. The last thing she'd wanted was a night-driving lesson, and she was afraid Diana's mother would be worried. They were going to be late returning, but at this point, she just wanted to get back to familiar territory.

"I can't drive anymore," Diana said as they finally turned onto a road that was familiar to Louise.

"You're doing fine," she said automatically.

"I nearly missed a stop sign, I couldn't back up, the dogs scared me to death, I turned the wrong way and I hate driving. I really hate it. I don't care if I never learn to drive."

Her outpouring was so pathetic that Louise wanted to comfort her, but she couldn't allow herself to buy into Diana's insecurity.

"You are learning. We'll get home safe and sound, and it's all your doing. I'm sorry my back road turned out to be a difficult route, but you did fine."

"I didn't. I hate driving." She wasn't going to be persuaded. At this point, Louise wasn't too fond of it either.

Jack invited Alice to ride along when he delivered the fawn that evening, and she readily agreed. She wanted to see where Jazzy would be living, even if it was a temporary home.

Was this how Viola would feel when it came time to send the litter of kittens to new homes? She was wise enough to put a limit on the number of cats who shared her home, but it would still be hard to give them up. Alice felt the same way about Jazzy. After coaxing her to eat and caring for her as well as possible, it was sad to see her go.

Fortunately Jack was experienced in handling all kinds of animals. He came prepared to give the fawn the safest possible ride to the farm.

"I just cleaned out the cage," he said, referring to the rear of the utility vehicle he drove on the job. "I disinfected it, but she'll probably still smell dog. Let's hope she's strong enough now not to panic."

"I think she's grown a bit since we brought her here." Alice was watching as Jack approached the fawn in the shed. "I have the formula packed in ice. It should last out the week, and Mark has promised to send more."

"The Bellwoods could probably use goat's milk when it runs out. That seems to work for deer. You don't need to worry. Sam and Rose know animals. The fawn will thrive there."

"I hope Mark comes up with a permanent solution. It will make a lot of extra work for them, and I don't want to strain their hospitality."

"We'll cross that bridge when we come to it," Jack said philosophically.

He was wearing his uniform: dark trousers, boots and a light blue shirt that made him look like a deputy sheriff. A patch over the pocket identified him as an animal control officer.

"It's so nice of you to do this," she said when the fawn was safely in the vehicle and they were on their way. "You probably haven't had your dinner yet."

She was much too agitated to eat until Jazzy was safely installed in her new home, but she knew Jack must be hungry.

"No problem. Alison is keeping pot roast warm for me—that is, if those ravenous boys of mine don't eat it all."

"Well, I'm still sorry you have to do this after a long day's work."

"I'll rest easier after we leave the fawn at the farm, and I'm pleased to know that you have given it the best care possible."

Jack drove slowly for the benefit of the fawn, and the trip took about twenty minutes. Rose and Samuel's place was set in lovely countryside. There was a large complex of buildings including a big red barn. The two-story house looked old enough to be on the historic register, even though the wooden siding had a fresh covering of white paint. The workings of a modern farm were a mystery to Alice, but she saw signs of activity everywhere as they followed a long drive to the house. She spotted a bright green tractor that looked almost showroom new, but she had no idea what purpose some of the equipment served. The overall impression was one of prosperity and organization. Unlike some farms she'd seen, there were no junked cars or obsolete machines cluttering the yard.

She felt comforted by the Bellwoods' agreeing to take Jazzy. She knew that they were the best temporary custodians for the orphaned fawn.

No one was outside, so they walked up to the house. Over the front entrance hung a red-and-green hex sign with the word *wilkum* in the center. Jack knocked on the frame of the screen door, and a petite middle-aged woman soon answered. She was wearing a white blouse, blue skirt and a red-flowered apron tied around her waist. The pretty hair that framed her face was brown, and her twinkling eyes showed welcome.

"Alice and Jack, come on in. I'll show you where to put the fawn as soon as I take a pie out of the oven. Come back to the kitchen."

"I can't tell you how much we appreciate this," Alice said.

"We've never met a four-legged creature we didn't like. You did a good thing to take it home with you. A lot of folks would just drive past and let it fend for itself. My pie has only about a minute to go."

Alice and Jack followed her down a narrow hallway to the kitchen, where Rose offered them a place to sit.

"What a wonderful aroma," Jack said, sniffing appreciatively. He dropped his voice to a whisper, "No wonder folks around here know her as the Pie Queen."

"I saw all the awards in your hallway. Did you win them for your pies?" Alice asked.

"The blue ribbons are mostly mine, but Sam has a bunch for the sheep too. The awards just keep spilling all over the place. I told him if he wins any more second or third places, they go in the barn. I'm working on a new recipe for butterscotch pie for the state fair. I'm not sure whether to enter that or stick with my blackberry cream pie."

The timer sounded, and she opened the top of two stacked ovens. She took a big glass pie pan out, tested it with the tip of a silver knife, pronounced it perfect and set it on the dark-green marble counter.

"Say, would you folks mind taste testing after we get the fawn in the pen? I'm always looking for unbiased opinions. Sam doesn't care much for the butterscotch. He thinks my lemon chiffon is the best one I make. Usually I lean toward fruit pies, especially when I can pick the fruit myself. I have half a blackberry in the fridge. It would be a big help if you two would try them both and see what you think."

"Well, if you really need a favor, I'll try to help out," Jack said, patting his midsection.

"I would be happy to sample them," Alice said, glad that she hadn't taken time for dinner.

She smiled and looked around the kitchen, which held a pleasing mix of modern cream-colored appliances and country decorations. The cupboards were blond burl oak with glass fronts, and large windows let in sunlight for little brass herb pots on the sills. The round oak table was surrounded by old-fashioned press-back chairs. It was a kitchen Jane would be comfortable using.

"Sam had to take one of our border collies to the vet. Otherwise, he would unload the fawn for you. Let's see what you've brought me."

They went outside, and Jack made easy work of unloading Jazzy, putting a harness on her to lead her to the sheep pen that would be her quarters. The whole complex was clean and orderly, convincing Alice that the fawn would get good care here. She felt fortunate to be leaving her in such a good place.

When Jack led Jazzy away, Alice had to fight to keep tears from welling up. By the fading light of day, she could see the warm brown of the fawn's fur peppered with white spots on her back, the baby deer's natural camouflage. The fawn's silence was heartrending in itself, a mute testimony to what the little creature was going through. Her legs trembled slightly, and she briefly resisted Jack's lead before following on sticklike limbs.

Alice's instinct was to make some gesture of good-bye, but all she could do was whisper best wishes under her breath.

"I have formula in a cooler and the bottles to use for it," Alice said when the fawn was settled. "We'll be getting more soon."

"I can't promise how long we can keep it," Rose said. "Depends on the fawn and on how busy we are, but be assured we'll do our best."

"I understand," Alice said. "We're just grateful for the breathing space. I'm hoping my friend Mark can come up with a solution soon."

"You said something about pie," Jack said with a chuckle.

"Just follow me," Rose said, leading the way back to her kitchen.

She settled them down at the table, and Alice began to understand why she was the Pie Queen.

"Now, if you're up to it, I have some individual pieces of my cherry surprise in the freezer. Won a blue ribbon at the state fair with that one. I'll heat it up in the microwave. It's not the best way to thaw it, but you'll be able to get a general idea. First let me whip up some cream. You can't have butterscotch pie without a dab of whipped cream."

Jack looked to be beside himself with happiness. It was fate's little joke that a man who loved food was married to a wife who was more interested in staying rail thin. Fortunately he knew his way around a kitchen himself, and Alice did give Alison credit for encouraging her husband to stay fit and trim.

Rose whipped the cream with a hand beater, explaining that it seemed to taste better that way. She added a quarter teaspoon of pure vanilla extract and a tablespoon of powdered sugar to the cream and brought it to the soft-peak stage. Alice was used to watching Jane in the kitchen, and Rose was every bit as professional with her pies.

"I like the butterscotch a tad cooler, but I think you can get the full flavor as it is now," she said, slicing off two small but not skimpy pieces. "Try this while I cut some blackberry."

"Oh my," Alice said, taken aback by how luscious the warm butterscotch was. The crust was so light and flaky that it seemed to melt on her tongue as quickly as the filling. "I don't think I've ever tasted anything better than this."

"You're not just saying it because I'm taking the fawn, are you?" Rose asked with a good-natured smile.

"She's a preacher's daughter," Jack teased. "You can take her word. This butterscotch is so good you should call it angels' pie."

"Save a bit so you can go back to it after the blackberry and the cherry," Rose said, taking another oversized pie plate from the fridge and slicing off two generous samples.

It took willpower to set aside part of the butterscotch, but as soon as Alice took her first bite of blackberry, she had a renewed appreciation for Rose's reputation. Rose's pie was extraordinary. She detected a hint of spice, perhaps nutmeg or clove, but she wasn't expert enough to be sure. Jane would love to have the recipe for it, but Alice sensed that Rose would want to guard the secrets behind her prize-winning pies.

The cherry pie was tart, but not so much so that it puckered the mouth. Alice loved it.

"We have three trees on the property to make sure I can get fresh sour reds," Rose explained.

She set out a big pitcher of iced tea to cleanse their palates between pies. Alice didn't see how she could possibly eat all three pieces, but the Pie Queen wasn't going to be happy if she didn't. When she'd finished all three, she didn't have a clue what to say.

"I've just eaten three of the best pieces of pie in my life," she admitted. "My sister is a professional chef and no mean baker, but I'm sure she would agree with me. I don't know how anyone could choose the best of those three."

Rose chuckled, pleased by her answer but still curious. "Which one would you give a blue ribbon to?"

"Easy," Jack said. "That's the best blackberry pie ever made."

"You weren't put off by the seeds? Some people don't like them."

"Didn't even notice them. I was bowled over by the flavor."

"I'll go with the butterscotch," Alice said. "It reminds me of the butterscotch candies my father used to buy for us when we were kids."

"So you're picking a sentimental favorite," Rose said thoughtfully. "If you didn't associate butterscotch with happy memories, would you still rank it as the best?"

"Yes, I think so," she said. "It's unusual, for one thing, and the crust is perfect."

"Butter does it every time!" Rose said triumphantly. "But neither of you thinks the cherry is the best. Did you find something wrong with it?"

"Choosing one of your pies as a winner is as hard as saying which of my sons I love the most," Jack said. "Impossible, and that's a fact. Your crown is safe no matter which one you decide to enter."

Alice murmured her agreement. When they left, she was carrying half of the butterscotch pie in a plastic container, and Jack had the remains of the blackberry.

"Feel free to check on the fawn any time. We'll do our best by it," Rose called after them.

Alice waved, then smiled a bit sadly. She felt sure that Jazzy would be safe and well cared for, but she was still going to miss her.

Chapter Ten

*J*ane could hear laughter in the dining room Tuesday morning. All the guests had gathered at the same time for an early breakfast, which made it easier to present her favorite cheese soufflé. She'd served it with steak strips and buttermilk-chive biscuits to their six guests: Ann Baldwin, a Buffalo salesperson, and two couples who were traveling together. The sisters were grateful for the prospect of a full house for several weeks to come.

Ann was at the center of their merriment. She had a gift for involving people in conversation and entertaining them with humorous stories. Jane was looking forward to a full day of her company. They were going to travel back roads and seek out small-town antiques dealers. Ann had planned a route that would allow time to "follow their noses," if they were so inclined.

It had been Jane's idea to pack a picnic lunch, and Ann had readily agreed. The night before, Jane had scrubbed out a cooler and put ice in sealed plastic bags. Everything was ready. All she had to do was add bottled water to the cooler and grab her purse. Louise and Alice would take care of everything else, including the breakfast cleanup.

Jane was relieved that the fawn was no longer the sisters' direct responsibility, and that Louise hadn't scheduled the third—and she hoped last—driving lesson until Thursday. It made it easier for her to leave with a clear conscience.

As soon as the guests dispersed to go their separate ways, Jane hurried up to her third-floor bedroom. She was dressed for whatever the day brought, whether it was poking around ancient barns or investigating dusty shops. Her jeans were faded but not yet ragged, and she'd compensated with a new summer top, a muted rose knit with a scoop neck. As an afterthought, she slipped into a blue checkered shirt, worn open like a jacket in case it was still cool outside. Her shoulder bag was packed with everything a traveler might need, including hand wipes, sunscreen, sunglasses and tissues. And cash.

Ann was waiting in the entryway, dressed in another long skirt and flowing top. Today her color scheme ran to orange and olive. She had a gift for making the most outrageous combinations work, and no doubt she wouldn't let yards of material interfere with her antiquing.

"Ready to go?" she asked as Jane came down the stairs.

"All I have to do is get the cooler. I'm not going to tell you what I made for lunch. It's a surprise."

"If it's as good as breakfast, it will be most welcome. So far, your food has been the highlight of my vacation. I've had no success at all finding postcards for my hunger project. Maybe you'll change my luck."

Ann seemed to have an uncanny knack for directions. She glanced at her map when they started, then drove confidently to their first destination about an hour away.

"I've covered all the closer places that looked promising," she said. "I hope you don't mind riding."

"Not at all. I love all the fresh green colors in the countryside this time of year."

The place Ann had chosen to begin their hunt was a large barn that hadn't seen paint in a century. They parked at the end of a rutted drive and walked up to the entrance marked by a large sign, Gruber's Antiques. Getting inside wasn't easy. They had to ring a dinner bell on a post beside the barn, then wait for the owner to come. He finally arrived after their third pull on the rope.

"Mornin' ladies. You folks looking for anything special this morning?"

A man with stringy gray hair, an unshaven chin, grungy overalls and a faded green plaid shirt unlocked the barn door.

"Postcards," Ann said.

"I got a bunch, but I don't keep them out here. You ladies look around. See what you can't live without. I'll go up to the house and get them."

All Jane could say when they stepped inside was, "Wow!"

"Wow, indeed," Ann said, wrinkling her nose at the great mounds of furniture, tools and architectural antiques.

An Amish buggy that had seen better days blocked one cluttered aisle, and Ann warned Jane against going near a pile of rusty antique farm implements. Jane spotted an assortment of frames leaning against an old wardrobe with one door missing and went for a closer look. She picked up a dark oak frame with no glass.

"There's no price," Jane said, looking at both sides.

"There wouldn't be. He'll look us over, check out the car and license plate, and see how much he can get from us," Ann said dryly. "Look at the corner of that frame. It's nailed, not glued or dovetailed. And look at the shine on that nail."

"Brand new," Jane concluded, returning the frame to its spot.

"See that table?" Ann said pointing at a round occasional table with an elaborate pedestal. "That's a marriage if I ever saw one."

"A marriage?"

"Someone—I'm betting it's the owner here—took parts from several damaged pieces and put them together. Just like he found some old wood and knocked it into a frame."

"I don't think we'll be buying anything here," Jane said, feeling cheated that what looked like a treasure trove included obvious dross. "Where do you think he gets junk like this?"

"Auctions, neighbors, even the dump. He probably keeps it cluttered on purpose so customers can imagine they've discovered something. If he has any good merchandise, it's probably in his house waiting for his regulars to pick through it, most likely dealers from a big city. I've run into more than one bottom-feeder like him. Let's go."

They stepped out into the welcome fresh air, but the owner cut them off before they could walk to the car.

"Here are the postcards. If you're interested, I can make you a deal for the whole box. Two hundred bucks. Must be six or seven hundred all told."

"I'd like to see them," Ann said, reaching for the grimy carton he held out to her.

It took her less than a minute to flip through them.

"No thanks," she said, handing them back and ignoring his wheedling voice offering to bargain.

Back in the car, Jane was a little puzzled.

"How could you tell so quickly that the cards weren't worth buying."

"They all seemed to be chromes from the 1960s and 1970s. They're supposed to have a nice shiny surface like modern cards, but those were all cloudy. Some manufacturers had trouble with the process, and their cards have turned hazy with age, especially if they've been stored in a damp place. I wouldn't give that old pirate more than ten dollars for the lot. It would be too time-consuming for me to restore them."

"You can do that?"

"I discovered a way to do it. Just spray with acrylic gloss, the same kind artists use to preserve paintings. I wish everyone would restore their smudgy cards from that era. It's not hard, but each card should be done outside or in very good ventilation. I couldn't sell them for enough in my hunger auctions to make restoration worthwhile. Of course, his price was outrageous. I'm sorry our first stop was such a dud."

"I enjoyed it," Jane confessed. "All this is new to me. I'm delighted to have an expert as a guide."

"Oh, I'm not an expert. I learn new things all the time."

The next stop on Ann's list was in a small town not too far from the first stop. It was an antiques mall in a large building that had once housed a corset factory.

"Usually every little cubby hole is rented to a different dealer, even though the manager takes responsibility for taking payment at the front. I like flea markets where you can deal with the people who own the merchandise. Makes it fun to bargain. Let's see what they have."

Jane was beginning to realize that antiquing with Ann might be strenuous. Considering how small the town was, the offerings inside the old brick building were extensive. Dozens and dozens of tables, display walls, and old glass-fronted store cases were arranged in a labyrinth.

"Everyone in town must be an antiques dealer," she said as they walked past tables crowded with everything from old hats to toy tractors.

"Not necessarily," Ann said. "A dealer will often rent tables in two, four or even more malls. If stuff doesn't sell in one place, it can be moved to another."

"But who will buy it in a tiny town like this?"

"Tourists like me," she said with a hearty laugh. "Dealers from bigger towns. Collectors who travel just to find things for their collections. If the malls advertise their whereabouts, people come. I guess I'm proof of that."

Jane stopped in front of a table covered with vividly colored glass pieces, vases and dishes in shades that enchanted her.

"Reproductions," Ann said ominously.

"All of them?" Jane picked up an especially attractive orange compote with an iridescent finish.

"They're made to look like old carnival glass. The antique pieces were inexpensive when they were new.

Tradition says they were even given away as carnival prizes or movie-house premiums. I've never checked on their history, but I guarantee these are repros. Look, there are three alike in this booth, not placed side by side to make it obvious."

"Some are pretty."

"Of course, and there's nothing wrong with selling or buying them, just as long as you know they're not old and you don't pay the price of an antique."

"How are these prices?" Jane picked up a pretty purple candy dish.

"That one may actually be an antique. Compare the quality to some of the others. But almost everything on this table is grossly overpriced for new glass."

"Out of my price range," Jane said, carefully returning the dish to the table.

She was soon drawn to a case of books with several shelves of cookbooks. Ann wandered ahead while Jane browsed. She found an old edition of the *White House Cookbook*, but since she already had a later edition, she passed on it. A book of recipes published in the 1920s by a baking powder company was tempting until she leafed through it. The original owner had apparently left samples of every ingredient she'd ever used on the pages. It wouldn't be pleasant to own such a soiled book, even if the recipes were interesting.

After careful searching, she did find a collection of recipes in a spiral-bound book put out by a Vermont church thirty years earlier. Sometimes these amateur publications were delightful, especially since each recipe was a favorite of the contributor. The cover had a quaint drawing of a cook at work done by a church member. Jane skimmed and found a recipe for nutty tarts using maple syrup, one she'd never seen before. The price was modest, and Jane decided to buy it.

Ann was frowning when Jane caught up with her.

"I wish I knew the dealer's code on this," she said, pointing to a cameo brooch in a locked glass display box. "My aunt loves them, and it would be a perfect birthday gift."

It was the head of a woman, a pink carved shell on white with fine gold filigree around the edges. She could see why Ann had noticed it.

"What do you mean by dealer's code?"

"Most sellers can't remember what they paid for every piece of merchandise, so they devise a code. See the letters under the price? Usually they just use their name or some other word that's meaningful to them. Each letter stands for a number. This one is HES. Let's see if the dealer left his business card on the table. Yes, here it is—Herman Davis. If he used his name, *H* would be one, *E* would be two and so on. *S* would probably represent a zero since it's the last letter in his name. That would mean he paid 120 dollars for the brooch. He's asking 250 dollars, so I probably have the code right."

"He's asking more than double. Do you think he would take less?"

"It depends on how long he's had it. Dealers can't afford to leave their money tied up too long. They usually need it to buy fresh stock."

"He wants to more than double his money." Jane was shocked.

"I know, it sounds outrageous, but it's pretty standard. A dealer can't stay in business otherwise. Consider that he had to buy it, possibly by traveling to an auction and spending money on gas, food, and even lodging. It might have needed cleaning or repairing, possibly by a jeweler. Then it has to be priced and brought to the mall with more expense for gas and vehicle maintenance. He has to consider his time, and he probably runs advertising, another outlay that contributes to the price of his merchandise. Add taxes and storage space for excess merchandise, plus the rent here and possibly elsewhere. It's possible if he were here, I could get the price down ten percent, the standard discount when dealers sell to other dealers, but he isn't here. It's beyond my budget anyway, but it's interesting to figure out what he had to pay."

"It sounds more like a labor of love than a profitable business," Jane said.

"Often it is. I had a friend who tried being a dealer for a year or so. She used to joke that she made about ten cents an hour for her time."

Jane left the mall, pleased with the cookbook and even happier to know that most dealers weren't like the unsavory man at the barn or the one with the overpriced reproductions.

"You didn't find any postcards here either," Jane said when they were on their way.

"I saw a lot, but unfortunately they were priced too high for my auction. If it wasn't for all the church women's groups that supply me with cards they've accumulated, I couldn't do it. But I was hoping to find a few good bargains to contribute myself."

They drove down the town's main street, two blocks of businesses with several stores boarded up. On the fringe of town Jane spotted a sign.

"Look, there's a garage sale. Should we stop?"

"My car stops automatically at garage sales," Ann said as she slowed and turned into a gravel driveway leading to an old house with peeling blue paint and a precariously slanting front porch.

At first sight the sale didn't look promising. An old wringer washing machine and two tattered puce wing chairs were among the sad-looking furnishings lining the drive. A little girl of three or so watched solemnly as they walked toward the garage. She had big blue eyes and wispy hair badly in need of brushing. Her nose was runny, and Jane had to suppress an urge to give her a tissue from her purse. Her mother might be offended if a stranger tried to offer care for her daughter. A baby was sleeping in a child's car seat off to the side of the drive, its face shadowed by a sunbonnet that had faded to a faint blue.

The woman sitting at a battered card table just inside the garage was thin and haggard with mousy brown hair pulled back in a stubby tail. She greeted them listlessly and invited them to look around.

"If you don't like the price, I'm willing to go some lower," she offered. "My husband's grandpa passed on, and I sure will be glad to get rid of all his old stuff."

"Thank you," Ann said. "We'll have a good look."

There was a musty smell in the garage that was off-putting, but Jane soon forgot it when she started sifting through the huge array of items on makeshift tables.

"Have you had a lot of people?" Ann asked as she looked over the tables with a practiced eye.

"Sold a fair bit last week, but my husband hauled another load from the farmhouse yesterday. No end to the junk that old man accumulated." Her tone told them how offensive she found it.

Jane passed up old license plates, a full table of kitchen implements and dishes in sorry condition and a huge stack of Styrofoam egg cartons. Then her eyes rested on a pair of oval frames with photos of a man and a woman in old-fashioned clothing.

"Look at these frames, Ann."

"Late nineteenth century by the look of them. A shame they were painted that ugly black."

"I would strip the paint. It's chipping off in places, and I doubt it's original."

Jane frowned at the price, twenty-five dollars for the pair. It was more than she expected from this kind of sale, but if she found old hardwood under the paint, they would be well worth it."

"You could bargain a bit," Ann suggested.

"Oh, I think they're worth at least that. I'm going to buy them."

Even though she liked the idea of being a savvy buyer, she didn't have it in her to bargain with a woman so obviously in need of money.

She held on to the frames while Ann finished a circuit of the garage and picked up a coverless wooden box filled with odds and ends of mostly broken jewelry.

"I have a friend who makes beautiful art with odds and ends," she explained. "She would probably like to have this."

Jane paid for the frames, offering to remove the old photographs so the woman could keep them.

"I got enough in-laws who are alive without keeping pictures of the dead ones. Thanks just the same," the woman said.

"I'll take this," Ann said, placing the battered old box on the card table. "But I won't take this."

She dug a large brooch out of the tangle of costume jewelry and sundry items. The woman looked at her blankly.

"It's hair jewelry," Ann explained. "Around the middle of the nineteenth century, it was the custom to snip a bit of hair from a deceased person and arrange it in a brooch or locket as a keepsake."

Jane could see a hank of gray-brown hair under what appeared to be glass. It was framed by an oval band of gold, but she thought it was a bit weird.

"It's not my cup of tea," Ann went on, "but there are people who collect hair jewelry. I've seen pieces offered for sale for several hundred dollars. I'm not sure what yours is worth, but it seems to be in good condition. I suspect the setting is real gold."

"Gold?" the owner asked in surprise, taking the piece of jewelry in her hand as though she'd never seen it before.

"Before you sell it, you might show it to the people at the antiques mall. They may have a dealer there who would want to buy it."

Ann paid for the rest of the jewelry, although for a moment Jane thought the woman would refuse to sell. She poked through it suspiciously, as though there might be other treasures hiding there.

When they were back in the car, Jane remarked, "She didn't even thank you."

"I imagine that she was just stunned that I told her the value instead of making off with it."

"It was nice of you to tell her."

"It was nice of you to pay too much for the frames," Ann said with a grin.

They laughed in understanding. There was more to antiquing than trying to best other people.

"Are you hungry yet?" Jane asked.

"Famished. Let's see if we can find a nice place for our picnic."

The next little town on their route had a small park with picnic tables and a pond. It was deserted except for an elderly couple tossing bread crumbs to the ducks. Jane brought out the cooler and spread a checkered cloth on a weathered tabletop, then unloaded the cooler and set out plastic plates, cups and forks.

"I made it simple," Jane said. "I hope you like shrimp and macaroni salad."

She unwrapped a long loaf of French bread that she had split lengthwise and buttered before slicing it into chunks.

To top off the picnic she'd brought a plate of assorted cheeses, green grapes and miniature apple-spice cookies.

"The cooler was getting full, so I only brought bottled water and diet cream soda."

"I'll try the soda if you brought enough for both of us."

"Plenty."

Soon Jane found herself laughing as much as the breakfast guests who had enjoyed Ann's company. As a lifestyle reporter before her retirement, she had ventured into beautiful and bizarre places in search of stories.

"I took one look at all those cages and galloped out of there," Ann said in a burst of laughter. "I told my editor I would go into the lion pit at the zoo before I interviewed a man who bragged about having 107 snakes. Can you imagine? Some of them were a block long."

They found they had much in common, especially a love for trying new things. Both were divorced, but they had come to terms with their status and enjoyed their single lifestyles. Ann regaled her with stories of an eighty-year-old neighbor who was determined to court her with bouquets of flowers from his garden.

"He's an old dear," Ann confided, "but last year when the lilacs were blooming, I had to use my scrub bucket to hold all the ones he gave me."

Surprisingly, the lunch break renewed Jane's enthusiasm for the hunt, and they set off to make more stops as they wandered along lightly traveled roads, gradually working their way back toward Acorn Hill. Ann didn't find any of the elusive postcard bargains that she'd been hoping for, but Jane found a stack of frames being offered for a dollar each. Most were in sad shape and lacked glass, but she found half a dozen worth her time to restore.

They were close to home in late afternoon when Ann spotted a garage sale on the outskirts of Potterston.

"Are you game for one more?" she asked.

"Their trash may be our treasure," Jane said in agreement.

The odds and ends offered for sale in the garage looked thoroughly picked over, but Ann spotted a rhinestone pin with missing stones being offered for twenty-five cents.

"My friend can usually replace missing stones from her accumulation," she explained.

They waited to pay as the seller talked to a pair of young men in jeans and T-shirts, one with a blond brush cut and the other with long black hair tied back in a tail.

"Do you have any coins?" the shorter of the two asked.

"My husband has a nice collection of early American silver dollars in the house," the woman said proudly, "but he would never consider selling it."

Jane heard Ann gasp. When the two men ambled away, she stepped up to pay for the pin, handing the woman a quarter.

"I wish you hadn't said that." Ann sounded genuinely distressed.

"What?" The woman had a sharp voice that rather matched her stern demeanor.

"About your husband's coin collection. If you're lucky, they're genuine collectors looking to buy. But it's dangerous to tell potential thieves what you have inside your house. Can you think of a better way to pick targets for a burglary?"

"I'm sure they're just nice young men," the woman said, nervously brushing a strand of bluish-gray hair back from her face.

"It's just something to keep in mind if you have another sale," Ann said in a soothing voice.

In the car, she wondered aloud whether she should have said anything.

"I just hate to see people putting themselves at risk," she explained. "When people put out a sign to sell things from their home, they have to be a bit defensive. Once I was at a yard sale where a whole bunch of people got out of a van and swarmed all over the things for sale. A man was working by himself, and one of the women engaged him in lengthy bargaining over the price of an old thermos. Meanwhile, the rest of the gang was price-switching, putting tags for low amounts on more expensive things they wanted to buy. As soon as I had a chance, I warned the owner in a whisper."

"What did he do?"

"Well, he was furious and threatened to call the police if they didn't get off his property pronto. They protested a bit, but in a couple of minutes, they were in their van speeding away."

"I admire you for speaking out," Jane said as they headed back to Grace Chapel Inn.

She was pleased with her treasures, but even happier that she'd learned so much about the antiques game from Ann.

Chapter Eleven

*J*ane didn't have a chance to talk at length with her
sisters about the day she'd spent antiquing until
lunch on Wednesday. Their guests had all checked out
except for Ann Baldwin, who'd left the inn right after
breakfast. They had time to relax for a while before new
arrivals checked in, a family of three generations traveling
together to Washington, D.C., who would occupy the
remaining three rooms.

Their lunch was a simple meal, cottage cheese and fruit
with toasted caraway rye bread that Alice had brought
home from the bakery after her morning walk.

"I was proud to be with Ann when she told the woman
about the hair brooch," Jane said after telling the highlights
of their trip.

"I don't imagine everyone would be that honest."
Louise munched on a bit of toast, not showing much
appetite.

"Probably not, but it made the day much more enjoyable for me. I like treasure hunting, but not if it means taking advantage of someone."

"I haven't noticed the frames anywhere," Louise said.

"I put them in the shed temporarily. Some need the paint stripped. I'm not going to work on them until I feel inspired."

"I am glad you took yesterday off," Alice said. "You should do it more often whether we're busy or not. You know the old saying about all work and no play."

"Our Jane will never be a dull girl," Louise said with a laugh.

"Here you all are," Ethel said, coming into the kitchen from the front hallway. "I have something to show you."

She plunked down an old shoebox and sat at the table with her nieces.

"You told me about your guest looking for postcards, and I remembered this box I'd stuck at the back of a closet shelf." She removed the cover. "I've had these old cards for ages. They come from my Bob's family, so I never had the inclination to part with them."

"They look old," Louise said, reaching over and pulling one out of the box. "This one was mailed to someone named Henrietta Blackwell in 1909. Do you know who that is, Aunt Ethel?"

"There were Blackwells on Bob's mother's side, but I can't place exactly who she was."

"I bet your children would enjoy seeing these," Louise suggested.

"I've tried to give them to all three of my kids, but none of them want to be bothered with old stuff like this. There's not a collecting gene among them, I guess. I'd kind of forgotten about this box until I heard about your guest and her postcard project. I wondered if she could use them."

"I'm sure she'd be interested," Jane said. "Are you sure you don't want to keep them?"

"They're just gathering dust in my closet," their aunt said. "Might as well be doing some good. Is your postcard lady here now?"

"No, she went out early this morning. Why don't you leave the cards here, and when she gets back, I'll tell her about them?" Jane suggested.

"I had in mind to ask her about a few of them." She patted her fiery red hair and straightened the collar on her lime-green blouse.

"I'm sure she'll want to talk to you about them," Jane said. "I'll let you know when she gets back. If she has time to go over them, I'll call you to come over."

"I've never met anyone who likes old postcards," Ethel said. "I'm curious about what people see in them."

"Have you had lunch, Aunt Ethel?" Alice asked. "We just finished ours."

"A long time ago. It's late for you to be having it, isn't it?"

"A little," Jane agreed. "We've been pretty busy."

"When I was cooking for my Bob on the farm, supper had to be ready exactly at noon. You'd think the world would come to an end if he didn't get his meal on the minute. That's a farmer for you. When he came in from working, he was hungry. Of course, he got up so early to beat the heat in summer that he was running on empty by twelve o'clock. In all those years we were married and working the farm, I don't think I ever missed getting it on the table on time. That's one of the things about the old place that I don't miss. Now if I feel like having lunch at eleven o'clock or two o'clock, there's no reason why I can't. Of course, I dearly miss Bob, but I don't miss cooking meat and potatoes every day by noon."

"That would be a chore," Alice said sympathetically. "Oh, by the way, Jack O'Hara settled our fawn out at the Bellwoods' place. It's only a temporary arrangement, but she couldn't have better caretakers than Rose and Samuel."

"Your idea of feeding through the finger of a rubber glove saved the fawn," Jane said. "I hate to think what would have happened if we hadn't been able to provide some nourishment for her."

"Yes, that is a wonderful procedure," Ethel said with satisfaction.

"I'd love to chat longer," Louise said, "but I want to drive around town and pick a good route for Diana's third driving lesson tomorrow. I've learned not to take her on any road that I haven't checked out first."

"What are you going to do after you've given the three lessons you promised?" Alice asked.

"I wish I knew. She doesn't seem at all ready to take another test, but I'm at my wit's end how to help her. Maybe she just isn't meant to drive."

"Maybe tomorrow will be a breakthrough," Alice said optimistically. "Well, I've been called to go into work this afternoon, so I'd better get ready," Alice said. "One of the nurses in pediatrics is sick."

"I wouldn't like your schedule, never knowing when or where I'd be assigned," Ethel said. "I like to know ahead what's going on."

"Shall I keep the postcards here?" Jane asked.

"You might as well. I really don't want to carry that dusty old box home again. Let me know when your postcard lady wants to have a look at them."

"I'll do that," Jane assured her.

Her sisters and aunt had been gone awhile when she heard a knock at the back door. She went to it and found Jack O'Hara standing there in his uniform pulling on one end of his handlebar mustache, a sign that he had something on his mind.

"Jack, come on in. It's good to see you. If you're here about the fawn, Alice just left."

"I just wondered whether she's gotten more of that formula to feed it. I'll be over near Bellwood Farm tomorrow, so I could drop it off. One of their neighbors has complained about a dog killing a lamb. I have to check out claims like that and talk to some of the nearby farmers."

"No, it hasn't come yet. Would you like a glass of iced tea while you're here?"

"Don't mind if I do. I've been on the run all day. I keep telling the county I could use an assistant, and they keep telling me there's no money in the budget."

Jane motioned for Jack to sit at the table while she poured orange-spice tea into a glass of ice cubes. "I made some chocolate-chip bars this morning. They're cool enough to cut if you'd like to try one."

"Best offer I've had all day," Jack said with a grin. "By the way, I hear Viola still has a kitten to give away. You're not looking for a little friend for Wendell, are you?"

Jane laughed. "I think that would call for a family conference. I'm not sure how Wendell would vote. He's pretty territorial."

"Just a thought," Jack said as he reached for a bar from the plate Jane had set on the table.

He didn't linger after he had his treat. It seemed everyone she knew was especially busy today, and if she didn't get her shopping list made, she might have a limited food supply on hand.

Ann didn't return until early evening after Jane had finished clearing the supper table. She was in the process of mixing up some pumpkin bread that would keep well until the weekend. Seeing Ann reminded her that she hadn't had a free minute to browse through the church cookbook she'd bought, but then there was nothing wrong with deferring some pleasures.

"How was your day?" Jane asked after she invited Ann to join her over cups of herbal tea.

"I took time out from antiquing to do a little sightseeing in Pennsylvania Dutch country. These lovely Danish pastries are from a bakery I passed on the way home. I thought you might like to serve them with breakfast tomorrow." She pushed a large bakery box with a cellophane cover across the table. "I don't want to interfere with your menu, but I couldn't resist them."

"That's sweet of you. Thank you," Jane said, admiring the luscious-looking pastries. "Are you sure you wouldn't like me to freeze them for you to take home?"

"Oh, no thank you. So far my biggest souvenir of the trip is the weight I've gained. It's back to salads and grilled chicken when I get home."

"You didn't have any luck finding postcards today?"

"No, I am getting a bit discouraged about that, but I'm having a wonderful time. My friend is going to be so sorry she had to miss being here."

"Speaking of postcards, my aunt brought some over that she hoped you might be able to use." Jane picked up the box she'd set on the floor away from her work area. "I think she may be willing to donate them to your hunger auction."

"Wonderful!" Ann began looking through them, pulling out several for a better look. "They're all old, just what collectors want to buy."

"I think Aunt Ethel wanted to show them to you herself. Do you mind if I call her to come over?"

"Of course not. I won't look at another one until she gets here."

Ethel arrived only minutes later, pink-cheeked and a bit breathless.

"I have so many questions about your project," she said, hardly noticing the cup of tea Jane set in front of her. "After people buy them from you in your auction, what do they do with them?"

"A good question," Ann said, laughing. "I think you have to be a collector to understand the urge to accumulate. Some people are nostalgic and collect postcards showing places where they've lived. Others have a taste for art and specialize in cards signed by their favorite postcard artists. There are hundreds of topics. I know of collectors who look for anything to do with ice cream, marbles, navy ships, rodeos—so many others I can hardly think of them. Santa and Halloween are favorites. Some of those are pretty pricey. Or they may pick a favorite publisher. An English firm named Tuck was especially prolific. Oh dear, once you get me started, I could go on all night."

"Actually, I was wondering where they keep them. I must have moved this old box a hundred times," Ethel said.

"I guess albums are the favorite way, although some people have special boxes or file drawers. That's part of the fun of collecting, figuring out a way to organize them. There are probably as many different systems as there are collectors. I know of one collector who had her husband build special wooden boxes to house over one hundred thousand postcards."

Ethel looked dumbfounded. "I never heard of such a thing. Is that a record for the biggest collection ever?"

"Not by a long shot." Ann was bubbling with enthusiasm for her subject. "In earlier days, mostly the first decades of the twentieth century, postcard collecting was wildly popular. People exchanged them for any holiday you can name, even Labor Day or Ground Hog Day. Greeting cards for those two are pretty rare today, but some like Christmas and Easter were made by the millions. A trolley ride to the other side of town was an excuse to buy and send a postcard. I've heard of collections that ran a million or more."

"My goodness! I guess people saved more of everything in those days," Louise said, "but I can't imagine a million postcards. You'd need a mansion to house them."

"A dear friend visited Russia on a trip in the 1980s. She'd heard of a collector there and managed to find him. I always thought she would make a good investigative reporter, since it wasn't easy to get away from an escorted tour in those days. He invited her to see his collection. There were no walls visible in his apartment, just rows of shelves holding albums with hundreds of thousands of postcards."

"Where on earth would anyone get so many?" Louise asked.

"It was an organized hobby a hundred years ago," Ann said. "There were collector clubs for people to exchange their duplicates. Sending them through the mail was especially popular."

"Like some people exchange thoughts and ideas on the Internet," Jane said.

"Yes, exchanging postcards was a good way to have contacts with people in other countries. Today postcard collecting is a worldwide hobby."

"I've never heard of such a thing." Ethel took a handful of cards from the box and started spreading them out on the table. "I think I remember a Halloween card here somewhere. Yes, here it is."

She pulled out a whimsical card showing a little girl in a witch costume holding a black cat and a pumpkin.

"That's a signed artist card. See, here's the signature," Ann said pointing.

Ethel held it close and frowned, then finally made out the faintly printed name. "Could this be valuable?"

"It could bring thirty to forty dollars in my hunger auction, especially since it looks to be in almost perfect condition. Damaged cards bring quite a bit less."

"Just for this little piece of cardboard?" Ethel sounded skeptical as she pulled out several other cards. "What about these pretty flowers?"

Ann shook her head. "Those are birthday cards and are worth less than a dollar each. I would have to make a large lot of similar ones to get a decent bid."

"I think it's prettier than the Halloween," Ethel insisted.

"It is a lovely card, but flowers are much more common. The value of a postcard depends on scarcity and demand. Lots of collectors want Halloween cards, but not many specialize in flowers."

"That's a shame. What about these?" Ethel pointed out several that were photographs of buildings and streets.

"They're called real photos. Local photographers would print them on stock paper with postcard backs and sell them in the town. Not a lot were made in the smaller towns, so they have more value, depending on the view."

"This one is just a picture of some women," Ethel said.

"A lot of family albums have photos with postcard backs. I imagine people would buy a certain number and send the duplicates to friends or relatives, just like kids' school pictures today."

"I guess no one would want this kind today."

"Some collectors do. They collect them for the period costumes. Look at the hat that lady is wearing."

"It must have given her a headache," Jane said, marveling at the concoction of ostrich feathers and fake flowers mounted on a huge platter-shaped hat. "And look at the fur muff on this card. I imagine it felt good to have one on cold days, when people walked or rode in unheated carriages."

"Oh, look, a card with a picture of a baby carriage," Ethel said excitedly. "My mother-in-law kept her old dolls in one just like it. I wonder what happened to it. I bet my husband wheeled it out to the trash when she passed away. He didn't have much of an eye for antiques. I think I should keep this card. Maybe put it in the family album."

"Do you know who this is, Aunt Ethel?" Jane asked, taking out another. "Goodness, I didn't know little boys wore dresses and long curls in those days."

"That little boy looks a lot like my oldest," Ethel said. "Of course, my husband would have had an absolute fit if I'd put a dress on any son of his. Still, maybe I should try to find out who it is."

"I told Ann you wanted to donate the cards to her hunger-relief project," Jane reminded her aunt.

"I didn't realize what was in the box," Ethel said in a hesitant voice.

"Tell you what," Ann said. "Why don't you take the box home and look over the cards? I never encourage people to give away their family heritage. It sounds to me like there are some you should save."

"I did say I wanted to donate them."

"You still can, if that's what you decide to do. But once I sell them, there's no way to get family mementos back. Much as I would like to use them for world hunger, I can't accept them unless you're absolutely sure you want to part with them."

Ethel carefully gathered up the cards lying on the table and replaced them in the box.

"Maybe I will take one last look at them," she said. "Thank you for suggesting it."

Jane and Ann exchanged an understanding look as Ethel left for home.

"You must have a hard time getting postcards to sell if you talk people out of giving them up," Jane said.

"Not at all. People are basically generous when they know it's for a good cause."

"Anyway, it was nice of you to give Aunt Ethel the chance to reconsider."

Chapter Twelve

*L*ouise was determined to fill Thursday with useful activities, but she still couldn't keep her mind off Diana's problem. Her dread grew as it got closer to the time for the driving lesson. It should have been comforting to know that she was only obligated for one more session, but how could she abandon her student before she passed her road test?

She was briefly distracted by a phone call from Rose Bellwood.

"Your fawn is taking the formula like Sam eats my pies," she said with a chuckle. "Tell Alice that the poor thing is making itself at home with no trouble. It's a pretty little creature, so delicate."

Louise thanked her for all of them. Then she hurried off to Grace Chapel to join other parishioners in providing a spring cleaning.

The afternoon passed quickly and pleasantly in spite of her worries. She found it immensely satisfying to dust and polish until the interior of the chapel literally gleamed.

"You've been quiet today, Louise," Florence Simpson said as the two of them were putting supplies in the custodian's closet after the others had left.

Florence had taken her job as head of the cleaning committee seriously. She'd arrived early in the morning with a detailed list of chores on a clipboard and a place to check off each one as it was finished. Her system worked well, but Louise had to smile at her costume for the day. Her head was encased in a green turban—practical, but not especially flattering—that covered most of her forehead. She was wearing a cotton smock that covered all but the edge of her dress hem with a bright jungle print. At least she'd left her high-heeled pumps at home in favor of canvas slip-on shoes.

"I've been too busy working to chat," Louise said, not wanting to explain how anxious she was about the driving lesson. "We've done a good job, don't you think?"

"Yes, although I'm not happy about that spot on the carpeting. I can't imagine how it got there."

"Oh, it's hardly noticeable."

Louise didn't want to critique the cleaning job. She was hoping to be the last one to leave so she could have a little quiet time in the chapel before going home. She felt trapped by her promise to help Diana and wanted to pray in the soothing atmosphere of the church. Daniel Howard had always impressed on his daughters that prayer was effective no matter where it was offered up, but she felt closer to God when she spoke with Him in this special place. When she gazed at her father's favorite stained-glass window, a scene of the Ascension in leaded glass more beautiful than jewels when the sun shone through, her troubles seemed to dissolve.

Florence was in no hurry to leave. She was a very active member of the congregation, and Louise appreciated all that she contributed. Sometimes, though, her take-charge approach could be a bit of a trial. Louise very much hoped that they wouldn't have to go over everything done that day.

"I was a little disappointed in the new member," Florence said. "I don't want to say that her cleaning skills are lacking, but I did have to redo several things she did. I think she was more concerned with finishing in a hurry than in doing a good job."

"She was probably concerned about getting home before her children did. She has three young ones at the elementary school. We have to accept what people are able to do, Florence."

"She could have said something before she left."

Louise didn't want Florence to get huffy, but she refused to criticize any of the women who had volunteered to clean. Grace Chapel was blessed with willing helpers who gave their time and talents to the Lord's work. Each and every one deserved gratitude. She reminded herself that Florence did too.

"You have high standards, Florence. Not everyone can live up to them. I appreciate how hard you worked organizing the workday. The chapel looks lovely, don't you think? You must be exhausted after being here all day."

"My feet are screaming at me to sit down," she admitted. "I'm not as young as I used to be."

"Well, thank you for all your efforts."

Once she'd defused Florence and seen her off to cook her husband's dinner, Louise sat in the front pew and prayed for Diana's safety and success with the driving. She felt her burden lift. Maybe this evening's lesson would represent a positive finish to her role as driving instructor.

After looking at her aunt's postcards the day before, Jane had felt a bit nostalgic. Uncle Bob's relatives had shared history with earlier members of the Howard family. Sometimes it was nice to remember the past. It made her grateful for her own life with all the advantages she enjoyed in this modern age.

For today, she decided to put aside her gourmet recipes and make a casserole that their father had often served to his daughters. By the time Alice and Louise returned to the inn for dinner, she had a big dish of Father's Folly, a hamburger-noodle casserole, in the oven ready to eat. She invited Ann to join them for this family favorite, and they gathered at the kitchen table to ask a blessing and to thank the Lord for all the years they had their beloved father with them.

"I love a good casserole, especially one that is obviously low in calories," Ann said, helping herself to noodles covered with layers of cottage cheese, cream cheese, sour cream, ground beef, tomato sauce, grated cheddar and seasonings. "It's so nice of you to ask me to join you."

Jane laughed, passed a plate of garlic toast around the table and settled down to enjoy the family special.

"Did you have a good day, Ann? Any luck finding postcards?" she asked.

"No, but I wasn't looking very hard. I'm enjoying your beautiful state so much that I wouldn't mind spending the whole summer here. Of course, I do have to go home eventually and think about earning my living, but I'm getting lots of new ideas for articles as I travel. There's nothing like a change of scenery to get the brain cells working."

"What are your plans for tomorrow?" Alice asked.

"I have to be up at the crack of dawn. I'm speaking at a church guild breakfast meeting. According to the map, it will take me about an hour and a half to get there. Don't plan on me for breakfast. Much as I hate to miss it, I'll have to grab something later if I'm going to get there on time."

"You're doing your postcard presentation?" Louise asked.

"Yes, the women there read about my project in a church publication some years ago and have sent a lot of cards for past hunger auctions. I'm excited to meet them in person."

"I'd love to hear your talk," Jane said a bit wistfully, still impressed by the enjoyable day they'd spent antiquing.

"Why don't you come along? I should be back by early afternoon, so it wouldn't take your whole day."

She pushed back the flowing purple and gold sleeve of her tunic to avoid dipping it in the casserole dish as she helped herself to seconds.

"Oh, I couldn't. We have a full complement of guests, and I'm planning a big breakfast."

"You should go," Louise said in her firm big-sister-knows-best voice. "You deserve more time off than you take."

"Almost everything I've planned for tomorrow has to be done at the last minute. I couldn't ask one of you to take over."

"You don't need to ask," Alice said. "I'll take care of breakfast. I'm not anywhere near the chef you are, but I did fix meals for Father that he seemed to enjoy."

Jane hesitated, not wanting to hurt her sister's feelings by pointing out her shortcomings as a cook. The inn's guests expected something more than oatmeal and toast.

"It's much too much to ask of you. Don't you have to work tomorrow?"

"No, I'm free all day."

"It's still a lot to put on you. I have the menu planned and the ingredients on hand, but I wouldn't feel right leaving you to fix everything."

"Nonsense, I need to learn more about the kitchen end of our business. We shouldn't depend on you for breakfast 365 days a year."

"I agree," Louise said. "I'll help Alice. You need to stop worrying about the inn and take time for yourself. We should be able to fill in once in a while."

"Take the whole day off," Alice said. "You know you're eager to hear Ann's presentation."

"I could point out that you are entitled to time off as well," Jane teased her two surrogate mothers, but she was pleased with the prospect of traveling with Ann once again. "I'm going to take advantage of your offer. I'd love to go with you, Ann."

"There's no need to rush home," Louise said. "What was it Father used to say? Oh yes, 'We'll hold down the fort until you get back.'"

"I'm so pleased," Ann said. "It's such fun to share my new experiences with you."

⌒

Louise arrived at the Zales' house a few minutes early and parked beside the curb. She was about to get out of the car when she noticed Diana standing in the driveway with a tall, slender man in a dark business suit. They were talking earnestly, and Louise didn't want to interrupt. She guessed that the man was Diana's father, and he seemed to be telling her something of importance.

The two of them moved toward the car, where Louise was waiting.

"Mrs. Smith, I'm Diana's father. I've been wanting to meet you and thank you for the lessons you've provided for our daughter."

"It's my pleasure," Louise said. "Diana's progress with the piano has been impressive. She shows great promise."

"Actually, I was referring to her driving lessons, but I assure you that we're pleased with her music as well."

"I have to take another driving test Tuesday," Diana said unhappily.

"You'll do just fine," her father said, "especially since now you know exactly what to expect. Your mother really needs you to pass this time, and I'm sure you will."

"I can't possibly take it again that soon," Diana said, speaking through the open car window to Louise.

Louise couldn't imagine that Diana would be ready by then, but she didn't say so.

"I've driven with you enough times to know that you've mastered all the skills you need," her father said in a kind voice. "The only thing stopping you from getting your license is lack of confidence."

"They'll ask me to parallel park. I'd rather eat worms. I can't do it."

"You did it just fine in the school parking lot," he pointed out.

"Without any real cars. What if I hit one?"

"We're insured," Mr. Zale said, "but you're not going to hit another car just backing into a parking space. Mrs. Smith, my wife and I really appreciate what a good teacher you are. We have every confidence that you can get Diana ready for her road test."

"I only agreed to three lessons. They may not be enough."

It sounded like a weak excuse, and Mr. Zale ignored it.

"I'll let you get on with your lesson. Nice to have met you, Mrs. Smith. I hope next time I see you, we'll be celebrating Diana's new license." He started toward the house.

"Nice to have met you, Mr. Zale," Louise called after him automatically, but she couldn't share his optimism.

He'd scheduled a test that Diana was almost sure to fail. It would take a miracle to get her ready by Tuesday. Even if they had a lesson every day until then, there was too little time, just four more days after this evening.

Louise worried that if she let Diana down now, it might ruin their relationship as piano teacher and student.

Diana looked dejected as she followed Louise to the family car. "I'm sorry, Mrs. Smith. My father just doesn't understand. I'm never going to get a license."

Louise had planned to let her begin driving at the house, but Diana was too upset to get behind the wheel right away.

As she headed toward the center of Acorn Hill, where she wanted Diana to take over, Louise mentally revised her lesson plan. Her student needed to parallel park between real cars. It was a frightening prospect, but the official giving the road test would expect her to execute the maneuver smoothly.

By the time Louise parked on Hill Street across from the Methodist church to change drivers, her hands were clenching the wheel tightly. If she was this tense about Diana's driving, how could she expect her pupil to be calm and relaxed?

"I have an idea," she said. "Why don't we get out and walk a bit? It's such a nice evening, I would love to enjoy the fresh air."

"You mean not drive?" Diana asked in surprise.

"Not right away."

"My dad expects me to be practicing."

"Do you feel like it right now?"

"No."

"I think the Coffee Shop is still open. I'm in the mood for a treat. Have you ever tried their fresh lemonade? Let's walk down there."

Diana quietly fell into step beside her. Louise took a deep breath and tried hard to think of a way to improve her student's driving. Louise would ordinarily have recommended the shop's wonderful pie for a treat, but the last thing either of them needed was a sugar high.

The Coffee Shop was deserted except for an elderly couple enjoying pie and coffee in one of the booths. Louise exchanged greetings with the waitress, Hope Collins, who came over to their table after they had seated themselves.

"I'm going to have a cup of tea," Louise said.

"Tea it is. And for you, young lady?"

Following Louise's recommendation, Diana ordered a glass of lemonade.

When Hope had served their orders, they sat in silence for a few moments. Louise was happy to have this quiet time before they attempted another lesson.

"How are the plans for the spring awards banquet going?" she asked, remembering a mention Diana had made about being on the decorating committee.

"We're doing a Paris-in-the-spring theme. We'll have a big Eiffel Tower in the middle of the floor and lots of streamers and balloons hanging from the ceiling."

Louise had asked the right question. Diana chatted happily about the preparations, forgetting her driving test for the moment.

"I'm glad you're making a big effort to keep up with your practicing even when you're so busy with other things."

"I love piano," she said.

They strolled back to the car after their treat, and Louise was glad she'd thought of taking a break. Diana didn't seem upset anymore. She buckled up, started the car and pulled away from the curb without incident. Louise told her to drive around Acorn Hill, letting her choose her own route. It seemed to help her driving when she didn't have to follow instructions. Her stops and starts were a little jerky, and she alternated between going much too slowly and a little too fast. But all in all, it wasn't a bad start to the lesson.

A car of teenage boys passed them, the stereo in the car booming loud enough to be heard for blocks. Usually she would have found it annoying, but this evening it put her own thinking on a musical track. She had one more thing to try with Diana, and now was definitely the time.

Louise saw what she'd been looking for after about fifteen minutes of driving. They were passing the library on

Acorn Avenue when a perfect opportunity to parallel park presented itself. A rather battered pickup truck and a little red compact were parked along the curb with plenty of room between them for Diana to park. It was a generous space, and no pedestrians were in sight.

"Stop here, Diana. We are going to park behind that truck," she said as casually as she could.

"I can't do it, Mrs. Smith. They'll just have to flunk me. I'm never going to get my license." She brought the car to a stop and just sat.

"Now, let's just pretend you did want to park in that space. What would you do first?"

"I'm supposed to pull up parallel to the front vehicle."

"Yes, and then?"

Diana recited the steps by rote and added, "But I can't do it."

"Let's take it one step at a time and see just what it is that you think you can't do." She ignored the look of consternation on her pupil's face.

"When you sit down at the piano, you look at the music and play according to what you see. Driving isn't so terribly different. There are rules to follow and a rhythm to it. Do you know what you do so well at the piano that would also help your driving?"

Diana looked at her blankly and didn't respond.

"Concentrate," Louise prompted her. "If you concentrate on driving the way you do when you're playing the piano, it isn't going to seem nearly as hard."

"My last teacher said that I didn't keep my mind on what I was doing," Diana admitted.

"At the piano, what's in your head as you play?"

"The music, I guess."

"Yes, and what are you thinking as you drive?"

"How much I don't want to drive," Diana joked feebly.

"Or what you're doing at school or about your friends. Now try parallel parking with absolutely nothing in your mind except the task at hand."

"I'll try."

She pulled up beside the truck and backed up swiftly, totally passing the empty spot without turning the wheel. The car was now parallel to the rear car but no closer to being in the designated spot.

"Now this time do it right." Louise spoke firmly, determined, even if it took an hour, not to let Diana avoid parallel parking. "You're going to park in that spot. I don't have any other plans this evening, although it might be easier to do it before dark."

Diana looked startled. "Do you mean I can't go home until I park there?"

"Exactly." Louise felt a bit mean, but Diana wasn't going to be convinced that she could do it any other way.

"Okay, but we may be here all night."

On the next try, Diana managed to get her car almost parallel to the truck's rear bumper before her tire smacked the curb. It was such a bad attempt that Louise suspected she was trying to make a point.

"Try again," she said without any other comment.

On the next attempt Diana turned the wheel in the wrong direction and ended up on the opposite side of the street. Louise was profoundly grateful that there was no other traffic.

"Again, but this time think of a bar of music. To do this correctly, you have to follow the notes, the rules you already know."

Diana gave her a look of sheer exasperation but pulled up for another attempt. This try was an improvement, but her rear tire still hit the curb at an impossible angle.

"You did a little better that time."

"Can we go home now?"

The teenager's brow was creased in concentration, and Louise could see the sheen of perspiration on her young face. Diana was trying hard, and it was difficult not to feel sorry for her and let her stop for the evening. But her pupil didn't need another failure. It was time for task completion.

"Not until you get it right." Louise felt frustrated, but she wouldn't give in.

"Aren't you going to tell me what I'm doing wrong?" Diana was pleading now.

"I think you can figure that out."

Louise fervently hoped her reluctant student wouldn't cry, but she steeled herself to resist no matter what.

"I have homework."

"Then you shouldn't waste time."

"Don't you want me to have time to practice piano?"

"Of course I do, but I know you'll get the rhythm of parking if you give it your full concentration."

"I can't do it."

Louise didn't respond. Maybe she was making a big mistake, but she was at the end of her resources. No one could teach someone who didn't want to learn. If Diana didn't make up her mind to park the car in the designated spot, it could mean the end of any chance to pass her test. She hoped it wouldn't also mean the end of piano lessons, but she had to risk it.

Diana did nothing at first; then she seemed to make a decision. She made another attempt, not quite successful but a big improvement over the other tries.

Louise said nothing.

She tried again and again and again. Louise lost count, but it had to be at least seven times, then eight and nine.

She was almost ready to believe that Diana was incapable of parallel parking when the impossible happened. Diana backed the car smoothly into the assigned space, then turned toward Louise with a tear escaping from one eye.

"I did it!"

"You certainly did!"

"Can I try one more time?"

"Try as often as you like."

The next attempt wasn't as successful, but she did manage to maneuver into the space about three feet from the curb. She tried again two, three, then four times, improving until she managed a practically perfect maneuver.

"I can do it!" she said, sounding exhausted but triumphant.

"You certainly can. Would you like to drive home now?"

Apparently Diana had used up her store of good driving skills because the ride home was jerky, alternating between too fast and too slow. She nearly missed a stop sign, and her brakes squealed when a car pulled out a good hundred yards ahead of her. But she did parallel park, the hardest of driving maneuvers, Louise kept telling herself.

When they stopped in her driveway, Diana's face was flushed with triumph in spite of the less-than-smooth ride home.

"Thank you, Mrs. Smith. I couldn't have done it without you. Can you possibly give me more lessons before my road test? I learned so much today."

"You learned to concentrate the way you do at the piano," Louise said with a smile. "Don't you think you can take your test now? All you really need to do is keep your mind on driving safely and remember the rules."

"Please, Mrs. Smith, I really do want to be able to help my mom. There are only four more days. If you could give me more help, I'm sure I'll pass. I know it's asking a lot, but you're my only hope."

Inwardly Louise was groaning in protest, but how could she let Diana down? She'd proven that Diana could succeed when her mind was on the task at hand.

"I guess it can be arranged," she agreed reluctantly.

Chapter Thirteen

*J*ane printed out the recipes we need from her computer file," Alice said as a sleepy-eyed Louise joined her in the kitchen early Friday morning. "Look them over and decide what you want to do."

"Other than go back to bed? How does Jane get up this early every day without completely wilting by noon?" Louise yawned and walked over to the printouts of their breakfast menu.

"It's nice that she has all her favorites on the computer, although I think that sometimes she cooks by pure instinct. One of the cooks at the hospital does that. She adds a little of this and a little of that, but the results are exceptionally good for large-scale cooking. I asked her for a recipe once, and she described what she does. There's no way I could duplicate it."

"We'd better get serious." Louise yawned again and measured out spoonfuls of aromatic coffee. "Let me think. How many people do we have to serve?"

"Seven, two per room plus one child. The Browns have their daughter with them."

"She looks to be around seven or eight. Do you think she'll eat what the adults do?"

"If not, we can always offer cereal or toast and jam." Alice opened the fridge and started assembling the ingredients on the counter.

"Oh dear," Louise said as she read through the recipes. "I've never made eggs Benedict. Do you think we can do this?"

"We told Jane we would."

"Maybe we should have asked what she was planning to serve. Do you know how to make the Hollandaise sauce? I always thought that was especially tricky."

"If you can teach a teenager to drive, this should be a snap for you. Now, the way I read this, we need to poach two eggs for each serving. That's fourteen eggs on seven split English muffins. The Browns will be down first. They asked for breakfast at seven so they can get on the road. The rest requested seven thirty. That means we can practice on the Browns and their daughter. We should have it down pat by the time the others come."

"Do you want to make the sauce or poach the eggs?" Louise asked, looking with trepidation at the growing assortment of ingredients. "I wouldn't mind slicing the Canadian bacon. It has to be thin. Eliot always liked his meat that way. He could make a turkey slice so thin you could see through it. I'm afraid he spoiled me. He liked to cook, and I was always more than willing to encourage him."

"He was a wonderful man," Alice agreed, sounding a trifle impatient, "but we have so much to do that I hardly know where to start."

"You had a good idea. We'll divide the jobs," Louise said, glancing at the clock. "I hope none of the guests comes down early."

"You can have your choice. The Canadian bacon came in a package already sliced, and the muffins are split, so that's taken care of. I have water heating for tea for those who want it. It will take awhile to make melon balls for the fruit course, but that's kind of fun."

"What does this mean, 'garnish the eggs Benedict with black olive cutouts.' Do we have to make fancy shapes with olives?"

"Maybe just little rings. Do you want to do eggs or sauce?"

"Eggs," Louise said, "if you don't mind. It's too early to even think about Hollandaise sauce. I'm sure it will be a disaster if I make it."

"Then I'll start the sauce, and you can butter the English muffins and work on the melon balls until it's time to poach the eggs. I think if you start about five minutes

before the guests are due, it will time out right. We can finish up the main course while they eat their melon cups."

Alice turned her attention to the recipe for
Hollandaise. It looked simple enough, perhaps deceptively
so, but at least the finished sauce could be kept over warm
water in the double boiler until it was time to serve it. She
tackled the first step, separating egg yolks from the whites.

"Do you think it matters if I break the yolk and get a
little white in the sauce?" she asked Louise, who was busy
scooping out melon balls.

Alice had to take a moment to rinse egg from her
hands. Jane never seemed to get messy fingers when she
separated eggs.

"It probably would matter to Jane. If the recipe says
yolks only, that's what she would use. Oh, and we forgot
that one of us has to set the table."

"I'll have time after I finish the sauce." Alice mixed the
bright yellow egg yolks with a little water, hoping she'd estimated right because there wasn't time to measure every little ingredient. Then she began energetically beating them
with a wire whisk over low heat on the stove. "The recipe
says to add salt and lemon juice to taste. Should I actually
taste it, do you think?"

She was talking more to herself than to Louise, which
was just fine because her sister was intent on forming

perfect little balls of green honeydew melon and orange cantaloupe.

"Oh dear! I should have read more carefully and finished melting the butter before I started. I would never make that kind of mistake with medicine at the hospital. Reading the directions is one of the cardinal rules of nursing." Alice pulled the pan away from the heat.

"I don't see why it should make that much difference," Louise said, reassuring her and also confirming that she was listening.

"Maybe I should have made it in the blender."

"I'm pretty sure Jane always uses the hand whisk. Do you think I should mix the melon balls in a big bowl, then spoon them into the dishes, or just put them in as I go?"

"I really don't think it matters."

Alice didn't intend to snap at her sister, but the butter was quickly turning brown at the edges in a pan on the back burner while she stirred the egg yolks and water. Discolored butter was totally unacceptable for a gourmet sauce. She rescued it with one hand, but not before she noticed that the egg mixture was forming lumps. After pulling both pans away from the heat, she had to take another portion of butter and melt it in the microwave. This necessitated covering the glass cup with plastic wrap. She was beginning to worry that the egg mixture was sitting too long and would be ruined.

Finally she had the butter at a perfect consistency, smooth and beautifully yellow. She put the saucepan with the yolks back on the stovetop and slowly added melted butter, whisking vigorously as she did.

"Something is wrong," she said after the last of the butter was thoroughly blended.

"I'm sure it will be all right." Louise finished the last melon ball and started clearing away the rinds. "Do you think I should put the melon cups in the dining room or the fridge?"

"I guess it's better to keep them cold, but I have a real problem with this sauce. Look how thin it is, thin and lumpy at the same time."

"What does the recipe say?" Louise walked over and began reading. "Maybe you put the butter in too quickly."

"I don't see how I could have. Maybe it was the delay. This doesn't look anything like Jane's Hollandaise."

"Have you added the lemon juice?"

"No, will you pour it in while I keep whisking?"

"Do you think I should measure? I don't have a clue whether to add a tablespoon or half a cup." She picked up a bottle of commercially squeezed lemon juice and stared at it dolefully.

"Just dribble in a little!"

"Well, all right." Louise shook the bottle over the pan, but only a few drops came out. "It's empty."

"There must be another. Jane said she had all the ingredients."

Alice watched with increasing dismay as Louise searched in the considerable depths of the large fridge and came up empty-handed.

"That's the only bottle of ready-squeezed, but I found a couple of fresh lemons."

"This isn't looking good. Hurry and cut one. You'll have to squeeze it into the sauce while I keep whisking."

Louise flicked seeds out of one lemon half and held it over the sauce. She repeated with the second half, but this time a seed flew into the mix.

"It's as thin as milk. We can't use it this way." Alice hated letting Jane down by serving something substandard, but time was racing by.

"It's almost time to start poaching eggs," Louise reminded her unnecessarily.

"I can strain it to get out the lumps and the lemon seed. The recipe does say I can put another egg yolk in a separate bowl and blend in the runny sauce if it needs to be thicker. I'll have to try it. We simply can't serve this."

"Speaking of guests, I think I hear someone on the stairs."

"Oh, I hope it's not the Browns looking for breakfast. They're not supposed to come down for at least ten more minutes."

"I'll take a look." Louise hurried out of the kitchen even though Alice urged her to stay and help.

It seemed to take her sister an awfully long time to determine whether the first guests were ready for breakfast. When she returned, she was flushed and agitated.

"It is the Browns. They've already brought their luggage down. They're in a big rush and absolutely itching for us to bring out breakfast. You'll have to poach their eggs and toast the muffins. I'll serve the melon balls and coffee and get the table set. Oh, and their daughter will eat whatever we serve. Her mother says she's not a finicky eater."

Alice poured the Hollandaise into the top of a double boiler. It didn't look like any she'd seen Jane serve, but it was too late to redo it. She turned her attention to the large skillet her sister used to poach eggs. Quickly filling it with hot water from the tap, she glanced at the recipe and saw that it was supposed to heat to 185 degrees. Jane had a thermometer somewhere, but she didn't have time to search for it. She read further and decided she would have to judge the temperature by the formation of tiny bubbles just below the surface of the water. There was no reason why that wouldn't be accurate enough. People had been poaching eggs for ages without benefit of modern kitchen gadgets.

Louise raced to the fridge to get a glass of milk for the girl. "They're gobbling up the melon balls as if they haven't eaten for a week. Mrs. Brown has a rather sharp tongue. I know I should be a good hostess, but no one has ever complained about our promptness. Are the eggs Benedict nearly ready?"

"You'll have to explain that they have to be poached at the last minute. Since they came down earlier than they said, they'll just have to wait."

"Oh dear," Louise said. "I don't think I can put it quite that way. Can you believe, that little girl found a seed in one of the watermelon balls and flipped it across the table. Her parents didn't seem to care."

"Remind yourself of all the wonderful, appreciative guests we've had," Alice said sympathetically. "I'll hurry as fast as I can."

She put the muffin halves in the toaster oven and hurried to prepare the eggs she needed to poach. Cracking them into a cup one at a time was slow business, but she had to be sure the yolks didn't break. The water was about right, she hoped. She slid the first egg into the hot water and watched with dismay as the white separated into stringy fragments. After scooping out and discarding the first one, she tried again. It stayed together but not in the nice round shape she'd come to expect from Jane.

Consulting the recipe between frantic attempts to poach the eggs, she confirmed the order of the ingredients:

two muffin halves per plate, a slice of Canadian bacon and an egg on each slice and top with Hollandaise. She'd completely forgotten about the black olives for garnishing. She was tempted to leave them off, but Jane always emphasized how important presentation was. With one eye on the bubbling water in the skillet, she found a jar of pitted black olives in the fridge.

"The girl won't stay in her seat," Louise reported as she returned to the kitchen. "She's going through all the drawers in the buffet, and her parents just sit and complain about the slow service. I won't be happy if our table linens get messed up. Please tell me I can feed them now."

"In a minute," Alice said. "Get the Hollandaise and spoon some over each egg. I don't know what to do about the black olives."

"There's no time to slice them. I'll just dump a few on top of the eggs."

The sauce still looked watery to Alice, but Louise put some on each serving and hurried to deliver it.

"Brown, remember that name," she said, returning to the kitchen with clenched teeth. "That man is smoking and using one of our china saucers as an ashtray. We've never banned anyone from rebooking, but we've never had anyone who had so little regard for our home. The child threw olives on the floor, and now she's refusing to eat what I served. Her parents just ignore her antics, and they act like we've served them poison instead of eggs Benedict. They wanted pancakes."

"They picked a fine time to make a special request." Alice stared at her less-than-perfect sauce and appreciated Jane more than ever. "I guess you'll have to take some cereal for the daughter. We can't send a child off hungry."

Louise went back to the dining room with cereal; she returned in a few moments.

"She won't eat this cereal. It has to be purple and red and yellow and green with funny shapes. Her mother is peeved because we don't have any."

"Let me handle this," Alice said resolutely. "We get children like this once in a while at the hospital, although at least there they have the excuse of being sick or hurt."

She walked into the dining room with measured steps, reminding herself that honey catches more flies than vinegar.

"I understand that you don't like our breakfast," she said to the pudgy girl with yellow pigtails and a scowl on her face.

Mrs. Brown, a thin, wiry woman with dark circles under her eyes and black dyed hair cut in spiky bangs, glared at Alice. Mr. Brown, balding and paunchy in a Chicago Cubs T-shirt two sizes too small, ignored her and sopped up the last of his sauce with a piece of muffin.

Judging by his clean plate, he hadn't minded their fare all that much. His wife was still picking at her second egg.

"I hate your breakfast!" the girl said.

"I'm sorry to hear that. Why don't you tell me your name and come into the kitchen? I'm sure we can find something you would like to eat."

"My name is Heather," she said, clutching the edges of the upholstered chair seat.

The child hadn't expected to be separated from her parents. She wasn't at all sure she liked the idea.

"We gotta get on the road," her father said. "I'm not stopping for snacks, so you'd better eat what I paid for here." He dropped his cigarette butt into the coffee at the bottom of a cup.

Alice had to fight the urge to tell him that all of Grace Chapel Inn was designated as a no-smoking facility. Even if the sisters had been willing to tolerate the habit, the fire inspector had banned it because they were operating in an old wooden structure. There was nothing to gain, however, by speaking out at this time. She could only hope he'd respected the warning posted in every guest room. She would have to check his room as soon as they left and give it a thorough airing if he'd broken the rule there too.

The last thing she wanted to do was hold up the departure of the Browns, so she quickly guided the girl toward the kitchen with a hand on her shoulder.

Louise had read her mind and toasted two slices of white bread. She was spreading it with peanut butter when the girl, less brazen without her parents' backup, came into the kitchen.

"There, Mrs. Smith has made some nice toast for you, Heather. That's the only thing we're going to offer, so maybe you should eat it like a nice girl."

The child gave them a look meant to intimidate, then sat down at the kitchen table in front of an empty teacup and saucer.

"I don't drink tea." She pushed away the cup, making the cup rattle on the saucer.

"Of course you don't, but at Grace Chapel Inn we think all our guests should use pretty dishes. There's no rule that says you can't use a teacup for other drinks. Would you like orange juice or milk?"

"I want double-berry energy drink."

"That's not on our menu. Milk goes best with peanut butter, I think."

Alice put the plate of toast in front of her and poured milk into the tea cup, then sat down across from her with a cup of tea for herself.

"My mother used to have tea parties for us. She told us to hold our cup like this with our pinkie sticking out." Alice wiggled her little finger in an exaggerated motion. "Can you do that?"

"That's silly," Heather said, but she picked up the cup and tried to hold it the same way.

They giggled at each other, and Heather began taking ladylike bites of her toast.

Alice talked to her about games she liked to play and things she'd seen on their trip.

"My daddy doesn't like to waste time getting places," she said solemnly. "I wish we could stop along the road so I can look for stones for my collection."

"The roadside is a dangerous place to look, but I think I can help your collection. Finish your toast, and I'll be right back."

Jane had recently spread several bags' worth of river stones to set off some bushes along the garden fence. It couldn't hurt to give a few to Heather to entertain her in the car. Alice picked up a dozen or so pretty ones and hurried back to the kitchen.

"You can take these with you as souvenirs of Acorn Hill," she said, "but first I'll rinse them in the sink. Come see how they look when they're wet. The water always brings out pretty colors."

Together they admired the smooth, glistening stones. Then she let Heather dry them on a paper towel.

"Heather! Your father wants to leave right now. If you haven't finished breakfast by now, it's too late." Mrs. Brown came into the kitchen with a scowl on her face.

"Look at what I have!" her daughter said excitedly.

"Oh, not more stones. Don't you have enough already?"

"These are special. They're souvenirs of Acorn Hill."

"Well, hurry up and don't bother your father about them."

"I'm glad I got to meet you, Heather," Alice said, solemnly shaking the little girl's hand and giving her the stones in a plastic bag.

"Thank you." She grasped the bag as her mother hustled her off without a word to Alice or Louise.

"Thankfully, we don't have guests like those parents every day," Louise said with a sigh.

"Poor Heather," Alice said sympathetically. "At least she's spunky. I hope she'll grow up to be nicer than her mother and father."

"I hope Jane doesn't miss her stones," Louise said with a laugh. "She does take her gardening seriously."

"They went for a good cause. No one loves a cause more than Jane."

"Oh dear, look at the time. The rest of the guests should be here in fifteen minutes. I do hope they're not early."

"The Hollandaise isn't right." Alice stirred what was left in top of the double boiler. "I don't think the warm water under it is enough to keep sauce at the right temperature. I have to make a new batch. You'll have to poach the eggs."

"I have to clear the table and put on a new cloth. We've never had guests make such a mess before. I don't want the others to come into the dining room and see it."

"Yes, you'd better do that first." She reached into the fridge and brought out the second and last carton of eggs, gasping when she opened it. "Oh no, this isn't full. Look, only three eggs left. Louise, I don't have enough to make another batch of sauce."

"Do you have enough to poach?"

"Yes, but I can't bear to serve this wretched runny sauce to guests. What should I do?"

"Menu change!" Louise said decisively. "One thing I can make for sure is a pancake. You clean up the dining room. I'll mix up some batter and see what Jane has to embellish them. I think she has some blueberries in the freezer."

"She was saving some real maple syrup for something else, but this is an emergency."

"Plump berries will make even my pancakes look festive," Louise called out as Alice hurried to the dining room.

By the time she finished laying out a fresh tablecloth, the rest of the guests were drifting down for breakfast. Fortunately the two couples traveling together to a conference in Philadelphia were pleasant people who wanted a leisurely breakfast with time to chat. Alice served the melon balls and filled their coffee cups, then went to see whether she could help her sister.

"I fried the Canadian bacon as a side dish," Louise said. "It got a little too well-done while I was turning pancakes."

She looked comical in a big white chef's apron with a dish towel tied around her head as a kerchief, but Alice's smile quickly died when she looked in the frying pan on the stove.

"It's burned."

"Only around the edges. I thought you could trim it."

"If I do, there won't be anything left."

"Then see what else you can find. Pancakes cry out for some protein on the side."

"Pancakes cry out? They're turning out okay, aren't they?" Alice asked with a trace of panic in her voice.

"Yes, I'm putting them in the oven to keep warm. They're not round like Jane's, but the blueberries should be enough compensation—I hope. Those guests are booked here on their way home too. I would hate to tell Jane that my cooking made them cancel."

"We'll hope they have a sweet tooth. I'm counting on the maple syrup."

Alice found a lone package of commercially frozen sausage bites in the freezer and hurriedly microwaved them.

"There aren't enough," Louise said frowning. "Three tiny sausages on each plate are going to look lost."

"We'll serve family style. Put them in a small dish, and maybe not all of the guests will want sausages."

"Then family style it is, but my pancakes always stick together on a platter when they're warm."

They looked at each other and laughed.

"Let's try telling the truth."

Their guests seemed to enjoy Alice's story of kitchen woe, and they graciously assured the sisters that the pancakes, misshapen though they were, were as delicious as they were filling. They checked out with smiles, promising to return and sample one of the inn's famous breakfasts prepared by Chef Jane, and Louise deducted the price of the morning's breakfast from their bill.

"We don't praise Jane enough," Louise said as they collapsed at the kitchen table for cold cereal and juice before they tackled the chaos in the kitchen.

"Not nearly enough."

Chapter Fourteen

*J*ane hadn't expected such a small church, considering the distance Ann had traveled to speak to the congregation. But what they lacked in numbers, the members more than made up for in warmth. The women welcomed their speaker like a long-lost friend, even though they had never met her, and they included Jane in their circle almost immediately. It was gratifying to be embraced in Christian fellowship. She was delighted to be there and thankful that her sisters had insisted.

She wondered how her sisters had done with breakfast. She wished there had been time to work out an easier menu, but that would have involved planning ahead and shopping. Her weekly list was still waiting for a trip to the grocery store. Eggs were the first item that needed to be bought, but she'd checked to be sure there were enough in the fridge for eggs Benedict. Well, Alice and Louise knew their way around the kitchen even if cooking wasn't something they particularly liked.

She soon forgot her concerns in the pleasure of being at Faith Bible Church. It was located on the edge of the small town of Sawyer, a picture-perfect community nestled in hill country with a main street that twisted this way and that through the locality. Many of the commercial buildings dated to a century earlier, and the merchants had been wise in restoring the original architecture rather than slapping on modern facades as so often happened. The stores and many of the homes were red brick, but the church was made of stones polished smooth by exposure to the elements.

"I've never seen a church quite like this," Ann said to Loretta, the guild president who was escorting them to a basement meeting room for the breakfast. "Imagine the work it took to find so many stones the right size."

"Our ancestors gathered them when they cleared the land to build the town. They wanted a church that reminded them of Noah's ark. That's why the front and back are rounded, and the windows are like a ship's port-holes. We badly need more space for Sunday school rooms, but we haven't found a plan for an addition that won't spoil the look of the church. For now, the older children meet at the minister's home for their classes."

The interior walls were covered with rough plaster with a slightly blue tinge, and the floor of the meeting room was covered with dark red tile. Instead of the usual modern tables that fold for storage, the breakfast was set on trestle tables of thick, dark wood that looked handcrafted. The ceiling was low by modern standards, and Ann seemed larger than life in the cramped surroundings. She was wearing another of her flowing costumes, this time a long skirt in shades of rose and magenta with a flowered pink top.

Jane understood now why she had arrived at the inn with an extraordinary amount of luggage. Not only was her wardrobe extensive, but she'd brought handouts to go with her slide presentation. Two churchwomen had volunteered to carry the projector and several packets of brochures.

The breakfast was really quite lovely, even by Jane's high standards. The guild women had made four egg casseroles with mushrooms and cheese, each varying in some small way depending on who made it. The church specialty was homemade biscuits with sausage gravy, made in the small kitchen off the meeting room. Jane often found this a little heavy for early morning, but the guild's biscuits were feathery light, and the gravy was delicately flavored.

"This is wonderful," she told Dorothy, the woman sitting next to her.

"That means a lot coming from Jane," Ann said. "She's a professional chef. People flock to Grace Chapel Inn in Acorn Hill to partake of her breakfasts."

Jane didn't want the breakfast to be about her, but she answered questions about their bed-and-breakfast as best she could. When the meal was finished and the tables cleared, she was happy to sit back with a second cup of coffee and listen to Ann's presentation.

Ann was quick and efficient in setting up her slides, using a portable screen the church provided. When she began speaking, everyone gave her undivided attention.

"Eleanor Roosevelt liked to say that it's better to light a candle than to curse the darkness," Ann began. "She took it from an old Chinese proverb that says essentially the same thing. The hunger auction is my tiny candle lighted by people like you who clean out your closets and drawers and send me postcards to sell. One little card is like one stone of your lovely church. It's only significant when it's put together with many others. Then your unwanted postcards add up to a worthwhile donation to fight the terrible problem of hunger."

Jane was as rapt as the rest of the audience as Ann ran through her slides and explained the different types of postcards, beginning with one from the 1893 Columbian Exposition in Chicago.

"In those days, only cards printed by the government could be sent for a penny instead of the first-class rate of two cents, so card makers bought US postal cards and sent them to Germany to have scenes of the exposition printed on them. Germany was the world's print shop until 1907, when our government put a tariff on imported postcards, making it easier for American firms to compete," Ann explained.

Jane didn't think she would remember all the postcard history in Ann's talk, but she was enchanted by some of the postcards on slides, especially a scene of little Chinese children in a mission school.

"Humor was a big part of the early craze for postcards, and trick photography was popular," she explained as she clicked to the next slide. "Here's a farmer harvesting apples the way you grow them in Pennsylvania."

She showed a postcard with a single giant apple filling the whole bed of an antique truck, and Jane chuckled along with the guild members.

"As I talk to you, children worldwide are dying from the effects of malnutrition. No one of us can end the horrors, but every one of us can do something. I know from the many boxes of postcards you've sent for my hunger project that this is a deep concern of yours. I thank you from the bottom of my heart and urge you to read the brochures about our work. They suggest many ways of fighting the horror of starvation."

Ann answered questions until Loretta finally stood to express the guild's thanks for the presentation. Even then, it was some time before they left the church, thanks to the excitement generated by Ann's talk. Several women had ideas for projects of their own, and the enthusiasm in the

room was a testament to their concern for the less fortunate. Jane felt buoyed too and wondered how she could be
some small part of the fight against hunger.

They were walking out the door when a feeble voice
called out to them. A frail elderly woman with a stooped
back and wispy white hair that barely covered her scalp
shuffled over to them and handed an envelope to Ann.

"I wanted you to have this card. It was my father's, but
I don't have anyone to pass it on to."

"If it's a family memento, wouldn't you like to keep it?"
Ann asked.

"No, I want it to go for a good cause."

"Thank you very much." Ann bent down and gently
hugged the tiny lady. "I'm sure it will fill a baby's tummy
somewhere in the world."

She didn't open the envelope to look at the card until
they were in the car ready to leave.

"Oh dear." She passed it to Jane.

"It's awfully damaged, isn't it?"

"Folded in half, badly soiled, the stamp torn off. There's
probably not a collector in the world who would want it for
free, let alone pay money for it."

"What will you do with it?"

"Buy it myself. It's certainly worth five dollars to have
such a poignant reminder of the widow's mite," Ann said.

"Your donors expect you to auction it," Jane said with a mischievous smile. "I bid ten dollars."

"You don't have to do that."

"It will remind me to look after the needy. Look, it's an old picture of the church where we just were. I'm going to frame it."

Neither of them was in a hurry to return to Acorn Hill, so they enjoyed a ride through the countryside, stopping several times at promising shops. Ann didn't find any postcards, but Jane found a small frame made of twigs glued on unfinished wood. It was just the size to frame the old woman's card. The frame was primitive, possibly made by a child, and the dealer only wanted fifty cents for it. She couldn't resist the unsophisticated work, and it would go perfectly with the folksy beauty of the stone church still visible through the folds and wrinkles of the card.

Ann hadn't located any good postcard sources so far, but she was a genius at scoping out lovely scenery and nice places to stop.

"It's all research," she said when Jane expressed pleasure at their lunch stop. "I did my homework online before I left home."

They were seated in an old post office that had been converted into a tearoom. The original postal window and rich golden oak woodwork had been restored. There were only a dozen or so small round tables, and it was a favorite lunch spot for travelers and locals. Ann had had the foresight to make a reservation. Without it, they would have had a wait of an hour or more, even though it was situated on the main street of a town smaller than Acorn Hill.

The menu was simple with only six main items. She and Ann both chose spinach-wrapped chicken with oriental sauce. It had a subtle sweet-and-sour taste that Jane was hard-pressed to analyze. She didn't embarrass the waitress by asking for a recipe that she probably wasn't allowed to give out. If Jane had invented something this unusual, she would be reluctant to give away the secret ingredients. She would try to duplicate it at home when she had time, although the sauce was going to be a real puzzler.

There was no choice of dessert. Every table received a plate of baked treats either to enjoy there or to take home. Jane did ask the sweet-faced older waitress to name the little treats.

"That's a golden apricot bar. It's tangy but not too sweet. These are caramel-nut cookies," she said, pointing, "and the dark ones are Dutch chocolate drop cookies. They're all made right here. We don't serve any commercially baked goods."

Both women opted to take their treats back to the inn.

"Alice and Louise deserve some after giving me the whole day off. I can't tell you how much I've enjoyed it," Jane said.

"I hope as thoroughly as I enjoy your company." Ann's smile confirmed the sincerity of her comment.

Louise had hoped for a restful day, but there didn't seem to be any end to the things that needed doing. She volunteered to shop later in the day, because obviously Jane would need ingredients for tomorrow's breakfast. Fortunately, no new guests were scheduled to arrive until late afternoon. In the meantime, the sisters had to hustle to ready all four rooms.

She began in the room where the Browns had stayed but stopped to call Alice in to see its condition. While there was no indication of any smoking, the room was a mess.

"How could one small family be so disorderly?" Alice said as she helped gather up fast-food wrappings and soiled tissues that had missed the wastebasket.

The bathroom gave them even greater cause for dismay. Heather had apparently used one of her mother's lipsticks to draw a picture on the painted vanity.

"Do we have anything that will remove lipstick?" Alice asked.

"I'll check the supplies, but I'm afraid anything that will take off greasy lipstick might also ruin the paint."

Her prediction proved right, and even the strongest cleaner left unsightly pink smears. The cabinet would have to be repainted in the near future. At least she was able to remove most of Heather's lipstick girl and what seemed to be a pig on a leash. There was nothing they could do right away; a paint smell might be offensive to the next guests.

It took more than double the usual time to clean the room that the Browns had occupied. Alice finished the other three before Louise put a freshly laundered blanket and spread on the bed and opened windows to allow fresh air in.

"Are you sure you don't want me to shop?" Alice asked.

"No, if you'll unload the dishwasher and do the dusting, I'll go."

Shopping didn't prove to be as easy as she'd expected, and there were three ingredients on Jane's list that simply couldn't be bought in Acorn Hill.

It was late afternoon before the groceries were put away and Alice was satisfied with the condition of the house.

"We forgot lunch," she said with surprise.

"No wonder I'm so hungry," Louise said with a laugh. "I can't remember the last time I did that."

"Jane always fixes it."

"True. Have I mentioned lately how much I appreciate her?"

"Not in the last fifteen minutes," Alice said with a broad smile. "Shall we go all out and have a peanut-butter sandwich...just like the one you fixed for that dear little Heather Brown?"

"Peanut butter with jelly, and I bought some carrots that are ready to eat."

"It sounds like the school lunches Dad used to fix for us."

"We thrived on them," Louise said. "But we don't need to tell Jane how much we regressed today."

They laughed because fatigue made them feel silly.

"I'm surprised you agreed to more driving lessons," Alice said as they ate their sandwiches.

"So am I, but Diana's father scheduled another driving test Tuesday. She's nowhere near ready, and I couldn't let her down. She really wants to be able to help her mother by driving." Just thinking about it made Louise feel even wearier.

"Oh, someone is here," Alice said, getting up. "Maybe our new guests are starting to arrive."

Louise followed her and was pleased to see that Jane and Ann had returned.

"Did you have a good trip?"

"Wonderful," Jane said. "How did breakfast go? I hope the eggs Benedict didn't give you any problems."

Louise looked at Alice and wondered how much to tell Jane.

"Let's just say it was 'Lucy and Ethel Meet the Preteen Bad Seed.'"

Chapter Fifteen

*A*lice was alone in the kitchen Saturday morning. The guests had finished breakfast and left the inn, and Jane was out working in the garden, something she enjoyed too much to consider it work. Louise had gone to Potterston to finish her food shopping for some items not available at their local grocery store. Since she was scheduled to work that afternoon, Alice was relaxing and enjoying a midmorning cup of tea. Certainly today was off to a better start than yesterday. They'd had a good laugh telling Jane about their misadventures, but the sisters sincerely hoped that they hadn't booked any more guests as unpleasant as the Browns.

"Is anybody here?" a woman's voice called from the front entryway.

Alice went out to see who was there and was pleased to find Viola.

"I never know whether to knock or walk right in," she said, flicking back a pale blue silk scarf with one hand and clutching a small basket in the other.

"Come back to the kitchen," Alice invited. "Have a cup of tea with me."

"I'd love to," Viola said, "but I can't stay long. I'm not alone."

"Oh no, you're not." Alice looked into the basket and smiled in delight.

A ball of black fluff uncoiled into a darling little kitten. She couldn't resist touching the soft fur on its back.

"Isn't he adorable? I still haven't found a home for him when he's old enough to leave his mother. I'm keeping a female from the litter for myself, but I'm way over my limit."

"You brought him here to seduce me," Alice said with mock disproval.

"Have I succeeded?"

Alice only smiled. "Let's have that cup of tea, and you can tell me more about the litter."

She was tempted to say yes. She would love to take care of a new kitten, but her nursing obligations made that nearly impossible.

Viola put the basket on the floor where no one would trip over it, then sat at the table as Alice brewed a cup of tea for her.

"How is the fawn doing?" Viola asked.

"Fine, I hope. Rose Bellwood called on Wednesday and assured us it was getting along well."

"Hello. Alice, are you there?"

She recognized a familiar voice coming from the side door and went to greet Jack.

"Jane said to walk right in," he said. "She's out there getting the garden in shape."

"Hello, Jack. Have you come to report on the fawn?"

"Well, sort of," he said. "I ... what do you have here?"

He walked over to the basket and stooped for a better look at the kitten.

"He still needs a home," Viola explained. "I brought him here for Alice to see."

Jack scooped him up in one of his large hands and softly rubbed the kitten between his ears.

"Are you going to take him, Alice?" he asked.

"I probably shouldn't," she said. "Jane has too much work already, and she would have the most responsibility for a new kitten. Also there's no predicting whether Wendell would take to him."

"You know," Jack said thoughtfully, "my wife is crazy about cats, but we always end up with dogs. I think a kitten would be a nice surprise for her."

"You'll take him?" Viola asked.

"Well, you offered him to Alice first." He stroked the kitten's head.

"I think it would be lovely if you take him for Alison," she said.

"How will your dogs feel about him?" Viola looked a little worried.

"We only have Roscoe right now, and he's as gentle as a lamb. I don't think it would be a problem."

"Well, if you're sure about not taking it, Alice, I guess Alison is getting a cat," Viola said.

"Have you named it?" Jack asked.

"No, I always let the new owners choose the names of kittens I give away."

"I guess my wife would enjoy picking a name. She isn't crazy about the name Roscoe even though I think it fits our dog." He replaced the kitten in the basket. "Just let me know when it's old enough, and I'll come by for it."

"I'm sure you'll make a lovely home for him. I love giving my kittens to people who are real animal lovers, and it's a relief to have all my babies placed," Viola said.

"Can I make you some coffee, Jack?" Alice offered.

"Not today, thanks. I've got a list of things my wife wants done. Actually, I was in the area and just wanted to fill you in about Jazzy."

Jack pulled on one end of his mustache. "I have a lead on a private nature sanctuary that takes in orphan fawns, but they only have room for so many. I checked, and they don't usually take any from outside their county. They're not unwilling to help, but their financing depends on local people."

"That's not very encouraging," Viola said.

"No, but there may be a way to work out this matter," said Jack. "Perhaps Mark Graves knows someone there. If you are willing to ask for his help once again, Alice, the folks at the sanctuary might agree to take the fawn."

"He is a well-known and highly respected vet," Viola said. "His intervention might do the trick."

"I'll see if he can help," Alice said.

"It's worth a try," Viola said.

"Here's the number and the person to contact at the sanctuary. I'll have my cell phone with me all day," Jack said. "Call me after you've talked to Dr. Graves, or you might have him call me. Right now, he's our only hope."

After her friends left, Alice hesitated to call. Maybe they were asking too much of Mark. He wasn't at all involved with local wildlife, and she hated to put him on the spot. Still, she didn't have a better idea. If Jack couldn't find another place for the fawn, who could?

Before she could phone Mark, she got a call from Samuel Bellwood. He wanted to inform her that Jazzy was doing nicely. When Alice filled him in on the latest development, he wished her well and promised to continue providing the best care possible until the issue was resolved. Alice thanked him for doing as much as he could, then made the call to Mark. He wasn't home or at his office, but she left messages on both phones, hoping he would call before she had to leave for work that afternoon.

A half hour later, he returned her call.

"Alice, I got your message. Good to hear from you," he said.

"I hate to bother you again about the fawn, but Jack has found a place for him. It's a privately owned nature sanctuary, but they aren't keen on taking animals from counties other than their own. I know it's asking a lot, but do you think you could make a call for us? They might be more willing if a vet asks."

"I'll be happy to, although I don't know whether I can influence them."

"You've examined the fawn. You can tell them the circumstances and assure them that it's a healthy animal."

"Give me the name and number. I'll get right on it."

After she talked with Mark, Alice realized that she didn't know exactly where the sanctuary was. Her fawn might be going hundreds of miles away. Worse, she might not be accepted at the sanctuary. What would they do then?

She tried to find a task to occupy her mind, but she ended up pacing the hallway, impatient for Mark to call but worried that his news would be bad. Whatever happened, she was sad that she wouldn't have a chance to watch her fawn grow into a mature doe.

Louise arrived with groceries to put away, and Jane came into the house just before noon to clean up before lunch. They were both sympathetic about Jazzy, but this was a problem they couldn't help solve.

At last the phone rang, and Alice rushed to answer it. She could tell by the tone of Mark's voice when he said hello that he had good news.

"It's all set," he said. "It's amazing what a small donation and a one-year family pass to the zoo can accomplish."

"You had to bribe them?" Alice sounded amazed.

"No, I only offered to underwrite the cost of care for a year. I always have several zoo passes to give away. That was just my way of thanking them."

"I'll be happy to pay for the care."

"Alice, it's a trivial amount. Let me contribute to a good cause."

"Oh, Mark, I can't thank you enough. I've been so worried about the poor little thing."

"Why does that not surprise me?" he asked with a soft laugh. "I'll call Jack O'Hara and give him directions to the sanctuary. I hope he's willing to take it there."

"I'm pretty sure he will be. He's been so concerned about it."

"I have an idea. They're open to the public by appointment. Maybe you and I can go check on the fawn when it's had time to settle in."

"Oh, that would certainly put my mind at ease. Thank you, Mark. You've saved the day."

"My pleasure. I wish everyone cared for animals as much as you do. I'll give you a call when we can visit."

After she finished talking to Mark, she hurried to tell her sisters the good news. Twenty minutes later, Jack called, confirming that he would pick up the fawn at Bellwood Farm that day and transport it to the sanctuary.

"You're welcome to come along," he said.

"Oh, thank you, but I have to work this afternoon. Since I'm the substitute, there's no way I can find someone else to take the shift."

This was one of the few times Alice wished that she didn't have to go to the hospital. Maybe, though, it was for the best. It would be terribly sad to see the helpless little fawn introduced into another strange, and perhaps frightening, place.

Lunch was a hurried meal. Ann had returned to the inn and invited Jane to go with her to a tag sale in Potterston. In turn, Jane had invited her to eat with them.

"The sale started this morning, so it may be picked over," Ann told the sisters. "But they advertised that it's a huge one with new items being offered as others are sold. It's supposed to last a week, and today is only the first day. It will be fun checking it out even if neither of us buys anything."

"Is it one of those huge old homes on the east side of town?" Alice asked.

"I don't know, but the advertisement said that the same family has lived in the house for four generations."

"It's sad that there isn't a fifth generation to keep the tradition going," Louise said. "Or perhaps the younger family members don't want the burden of a huge house. I know we would have been hard-pressed to keep our father's home if we hadn't turned it into a bed-and-breakfast."

"Yes, we're fortunate to be able to have a business here and still live in the house," Alice agreed. "I would hate to see all our family heirlooms stripped away in a tag sale or auction. Imagine how desolate the house would seem if all the furnishings and mementos were carried away."

"It's not the house itself that's important," Louise agreed. "The memories are what make a place special."

After Louise asked a blessing, Jane passed the bowl of spinach salad. For a quick meal it was exceptionally tasty with slivered almonds and a special dressing, but all of them were too intent on their afternoon activities to have seconds. They didn't even finish the plate of bacon-and-cheese points that Jane had prepared under the stove broiler.

Alice excused herself to get ready for work. She had a few errands in Potterston before beginning her shift at the hospital. Jane and Ann were eager to get to the tag sale, but Louise seemed in a somber mood.

"Is everything all right?" Jane asked her after Ann had gone to her room to freshen up for their afternoon excursion.

"Yes. I'm sorry to be so glum. Diana and I are having another lesson this afternoon, but it won't be enough to get her ready by Tuesday."

"Maybe she should postpone the driving test."

"She would love to, but her father thinks she's ready after all the lessons she's had. He can't understand why she's having so much trouble when she's such a bright girl in other ways."

"You said she finally mastered parallel parking. That's a big accomplishment."

"Yes, but her street driving is erratic. She finds it hard to maintain a steady speed. Sometimes she remembers the rules, and other times her mind is miles away. She'll stop halfway through a stop sign, or she'll slam on the brakes five car lengths before it's necessary. And I can't get her to pay attention to cars behind her. Now I know why driver-training cars have signs on the roof to warn other motorists."

"She may surprise you and come through the test with flying colors," Jane said optimistically.

"I pray she does, but I don't know where the girl's head is when she's driving. She simply doesn't keep her mind on the task at hand. It's almost as if she's programmed herself to fail. She says that she wants to help her mother by getting her license, but she may not be able to."

"Maybe Diana has to find a solution herself," Jane said to comfort her sister. "You can only give her the opportunity to practice."

"Yes, but you know me. I can't let a problem rest until I've found a solution."

"Well, good luck. I'll see you at dinnertime. I've invited Aunt Ethel to join us, but I have everything planned. If you get back before I do, just kick off your shoes and relax. Tonight's guests have all checked in, and there's nothing urgent that needs doing."

"What an angel you are," Louise said with a grateful smile.

Louise drove to Diana's house with a growing sense of dread that only deepened when she saw Mrs. Zale in the front yard with her daughter. Lara was dressed in khaki pants and an oversized green T-shirt and had obviously been trimming bushes in front of the house. At the moment, however, she was absorbed in conversation with Diana. Louise watched without getting out of the car, not wanting to interrupt their discussion.

Lara saw her first and started walking toward Louise.

"I want to thank you again for all you've done for Diana," she said. "I'm afraid my daughter has decided that there's no point in more lessons. She's given up on getting her license."

Louise was genuinely surprised. She was only at the Zales' home because Diana had desperately sought more lessons before her test on Tuesday. They had agreed on this lesson and a final one on Monday. As much as Louise would like to be excused from them, she wasn't willing to give up at this point. Something must have happened to change Diana's mind.

"I'll talk to her," she said resolutely, not paying heed to Lara's weak protest that it was of no use. "I wonder if I could trouble you for a drink of water."

"Yes, of course. I'm really sorry I didn't call and save you a trip out here. It's something of a last-minute decision. I'll get that water for you."

After she went into the house, Louise approached Diana, who looked far from being at ease.

"Have you canceled your driving test?"

Diana didn't answer.

"If I thought you were incapable of mastering an automobile, I wouldn't have encouraged you." She felt the need to speak frankly.

"I'm sorry," Diana said meekly. "I didn't mean to put you to any trouble."

"Well, you have, but it was for a good cause. It's important to you and to your family that you're able to drive. What if one of your brothers became hurt or sick while your father was out of town? How would he get to the doctor?"

"Our neighbors will help."

"You can't be sure they'll be home and available. A family has to look out for its loved ones. I don't know what I would have done when my husband died if I hadn't been able to drive myself to the places I needed to go."

"I try to help my mom."

"I'm sure you do, but this isn't just about your family. You know in your heart that you can drive. You've let fear and doubt take over. If you decide to give up now, you'll be diminished in your own estimation. It could be years before you regain enough confidence to try again. I've known women who never became drivers just because of minor setbacks when they were learning. They spend their whole lives depending on other people to take them places."

"I won't be like that. I'll learn to drive someday."

Louise shook her head sadly.

"I'm not a quitter." Diana sounded close to tears.

"Then get the car keys, and we'll have another lesson."

"All right, but it won't make any difference." She ran into the house through the garage entrance to get the keys.

Lara, meanwhile, came out the front door with a glass of water, and Louise told her that the lesson was still on.

She slowly sipped the water while Mrs. Zale stood by, neither of them knowing what else to say about Diana's driving.

For a while, Louise thought she had failed to reach Diana. It was taking her so long to get the keys and her learner's permit that Louise was afraid she wouldn't return at all. Then, to her relief, the girl came out through the open door of the garage. Without saying a word, she got into the driver's seat of the car and waited for Louise to join her on the passenger side.

"I'll go inside now," Lara said, perhaps sensitive to her daughter's concerns about pulling away smoothly.

It was the first time Diana had taken the wheel without prompting from Louise. When her mother was out of sight, she slowly and carefully drove out of her neighborhood.

"Where do you want me to go?"

"Why don't you decide?"

"Then we'll go to Potterston."

Louise was surprised that Diana was willing to go on the busiest road outside of Acorn Hill, but she didn't comment.

She drove through the subdivision using reasonable care and avoided slamming her brakes at the stop sign. Louise clenched her lips when they turned onto the highway, trying not to imagine all the things that could go wrong. She was acutely aware that the situation was beyond her control. What could she possibly say that Diana didn't already know? Maybe it was more a distraction than a help to have a teacher beside her giving instructions as she drove.

Louise forced herself to stay mute while Diana drove to Potterston. Traffic was blessedly light this Saturday afternoon, and it was some time before she came up behind a slow-moving farm truck. Louise waited to see what her pupil's decision would be, either to crawl along behind the pokey vehicle or risk passing.

"I hate passing," Diana said under her breath. "I hate it, hate it, hate it."

Still Louise refused to comment.

"It should be against the law to drive that slow," Diana said. "I should just turn around and go home."

The temptation to launch into a lecture was so great that Louise found herself biting her lip.

"Now," Diana said in a triumphant tone.

She pulled out and executed a reasonably good pass, allowing plenty of space in front of the truck before she went back into the right lane.

"That was well done." Louise praised her but didn't make any other comment.

The rest of the trip to Potterston was far from error-free, but Louise kept her resolve to let Diana drive without instructions. Diana asked permission to stop at a discount store and purchase a few things she needed, and Louise was glad to get out of the car for a few minutes. Her knees were shaky from the stress of riding silently with her student driver. She treated Diana to a diet cola at the snack bar in the store, then readied herself for the return trip.

The whole excursion had lasted less than an hour and a half, but Louise felt as if she'd just made an extremely long trip. At the Zales' house, she confirmed the time for their last lesson on Monday. Diana agreed readily and thanked her. It was a relief that Lara was nowhere in sight. The last thing she wanted to do was give a progress report on today's lesson. Diana had shown improvement, but Louise still had serious doubts about the driving test.

"There's no place like home," Louise said aloud when she finally reached the comfortable atmosphere of Grace Chapel Inn.

Chapter Sixteen

As soon as Jane saw the house on Gilbert Street in Potterston, she knew the trip was more than worthwhile. Even without a tag sale in progress, the late Victorian mansion would be a magnet for her curiosity. She couldn't wait to see the interior of the massive home.

"I can see why a family member might be intimidated by the upkeep," Ann said as they stood on the sidewalk looking at the turrets, towers, balconies and porches that seemed to have sprouted like wild mushrooms in a field.

"The builder must have made his master plan after collecting parts from medieval castles, Italian villas and French palaces." Jane stared up at the steep roof, asymmetrical windows, gables and dormers that contributed to the combination of architectural styles. "Look at that cupola. It reminds me of a witch's hat."

"It's Gothic at its best—or worst." Ann gave a mock shudder. "A kid would have to be brave to go up to that door alone on Halloween."

"Imagine living here. It's easily twice the size of Grace Chapel Inn."

"In our town, most of the old homes this large have been torn down or converted to apartments or businesses." Ann pushed up the sleeves of her unusually conservative tan-and-white tunic worn over a long cocoa-brown skirt, a signal that she was ready to get down to the business of treasure hunting.

As they went up the walkway to a door with metal rivets meant to make it look medieval, the condition of the exterior became more obvious. The narrow wood siding that covered most of the facade had faded, and much of it revealed peeling lavender-gray paint. The trim around the windows was a dirty yellow-white. Jane guessed that it hadn't had fresh paint in twenty or thirty years, and she couldn't help noticing remnants of black roof shingles that had blown down into the sparse grass of the yard. The artist in her thought of things that could be done to revive the century-old giant, but the task would be beyond her. No wonder the family was selling out.

"If we'd been here this morning, we would have had to take a number and wait our turn," Ann said. "They only allowed so many buyers at a time to go inside. I'm not very patient about lines, so I decided to wait. I like looking at the house as much as hunting for things to buy."

"Me too," Jane agreed. "Unless they have some interesting cookbooks, there's not much I want. It will take me a while to refurbish the frames I've already bought."

The door was thick and heavy with three brass hinges instead of the usual two. The knob, the mailbox attached to the wall beside it and all the other fittings appeared to be bronze with a pleasing patina. A printed sign on the door invited them to walk in for the sale.

The inside of the house was a maze of rooms with enough twists and turns to confuse a visitor. Some rooms had tables of small items watched by salespeople, while others were largely stripped bare or contained only odd pieces of furniture. There were still enough buyers to make it difficult to get close to the more interesting displays, so Ann suggested they start at the top. They were at the back of the house by then, and the closest stairway led off a pantry the size of a modern living room.

"The servants had to use these," Ann said as they climbed the steep, narrow steps. "Can you imagine running up and down all day carrying who knows what? These big houses are intriguing, but it's always a little depressing to think how many underpaid, overworked women it took to keep them up. Most of the mansions started going downhill during World War II, when women could get better-paying jobs in factories and businesses."

After a steep climb to the second floor, they came out in a huge open space that had once been the ballroom. The hardwood floor was pitted and dull now, and the fancy moldings above faded emerald-and-cream wallpaper were broken and crumbling from dampness. In her mind, Jane could imagine how it would look restored to its former beauty. She would love working on it, making a ruined room into a place of allure, but replacing the fancy plaster-work would require an expert. Most likely it would be stripped away, not repaired, if new owners planned to convert the house to some other use.

They wandered from the ballroom down hallways with enough bedrooms to start a hotel. These rooms were empty of furnishings for the most part, all the contents removed to be sold on the first floor. Still, Jane reveled in wandering through the past in the antiquated passageways and suites of rooms. She found a nursery with fairy-tale scenes on the walls in colorful but disintegrating paint. Her fingers itched to repaint them as they used to be. If she didn't love her work at their bed-and-breakfast, she could easily throw herself into the restoration business.

Ann's visit had opened new vistas for Jane and teased her imagination to be more creative in her own life. Creativity was all about ideas, not hauling home castoffs. She realized that among the real treasures in her life was the opportunity to meet so many new and interesting guests who came to the inn. Her life was doubly blessed by faith and family, but getting to know a vibrant person like Ann was certainly icing on her cake.

"You're quiet today," Ann said without sounding critical.

"I've been restoring the house in my mind," Jane said with a laugh. "Can you imagine what a huge job it would be?"

"It's my idea of a nightmare. Hanging a picture straight is a task beyond my mechanical skills. Fortunately my condo comes with a handyman to keep up the outside. I make most of my own clothes, but give me a hammer, and my finger will need bandaging. I oiled my old sewing machine once and set it on fire. Fortunately I'd only paid five dollars for it at a garage sale. I have a better one now."

They wandered down to the first floor, where a lively crowd was still examining the multitude of items for sale.

"This is being run by a professional dealer, someone who specializes in tag sales," Ann said.

"Does that mean the prices will be higher?" Jane asked.

"Not necessarily. I've been at sales where the family was so attached to the things they were selling that the prices were sky-high. Auctions can be that way too. As soon as it becomes apparent that family and friends are bidding on all the good lots at an estate sale, I usually go home. Sentiment ups the prices out of my range. I would rather deal with pros who know what things are worth. Let's see if we can scout out any postcards."

They checked the parlor, music room, study, library and a number of rooms whose original purposes were unclear. True to the advertising, there were still enough items for sale to interest almost any bargain hunter. A woman in charge of one room told them that the family also owned an old farmhouse, the contents of which were slowly being added to the sale.

"What are they going to do with this house?" Jane asked the question that had been on her mind since first seeing it.

"It's going to be converted to commercial use. I think a group of lawyers will take over the ground floor and rent offices upstairs."

"So it will be restored?" Jane asked.

"Renovated to their needs, I imagine. I don't know how much of the original interior will be preserved," the gray-haired dealer said a bit wistfully. "It is fun to imagine living here when it was first built, isn't it?"

Jane smiled in agreement. "That's exactly what I've been doing."

"Do you have any postcards," Ann asked.

"Not that I've noticed, but there are some boxes of paper items in the kitchen. You could check there."

A bored looking young man with a buzz cut and wearing a black T-shirt was perched on a stool by a counter in the kitchen.

"Look around, ladies," he said in an uninterested voice.

"The lady in the parlor said to ask here about post-cards," Ann said.

"Did she say there are some here?" he asked. "I'm just helping out while my mother takes a break. You'll have to look around yourself."

Jane was already poking in some boxes of clutter shoved under the chrome-legged kitchen table. There were old family photos, bills, newspapers, magazines and road maps. Ann started searching another box and came up with a handful of modern-looking postcards.

"How much are these?" she asked, extending them for the young man to see.

"Nobody wants those," he said rather scornfully. "Collectors want the old ones from the early 1900s."

"Yes, but how much are these?" Ann asked rather insistently.

"What do you want to pay?"

Jane hated to play this game, much preferring a set price that she could accept or reject. She was inclined to walk away when a seller wanted to bargain.

"Five dollars for the box," Ann said without hesitation.

"You're wasting your money, but my mother said to get rid of everything. What are you going to do with all that junk?"

"I haven't decided." Ann's voice indicated that she didn't appreciate his patronizing tone, but she handed over a five-dollar bill and scooped up the corrugated cardboard box, heedless of its dusty condition.

Puzzled, Jane followed Ann out to the car where she was quick to stow the box on the floor of the backseat before she slipped behind the wheel.

"Were there some old ones in the bottom of the box?" Jane asked, remembering that much of Ann's presentation had been about cards from the early twentieth century.

"Not that I saw, but there are collectors for cards of all ages if they have some historical value. Apparently the person who owned them was a space fan. There are cards from the beginning of the moon flights. I caught a glimpse of one showing Neil Armstrong and his crew. The caption said they were the astronauts scheduled to go to the moon."

"So that's a really valuable card?"

"No, not yet, but future generations may think of the Apollo missions the way we think of Columbus. The cards probably won't sell for much more than I paid, but I like the idea of putting them in the hands of collectors who will appreciate them."

Her curiosity piqued, Jane reached back into the box that was sitting behind the driver's seat and pulled out a handful of cards.

"Some came from the space museum in Washington. Don't you think they're pretty common? A lot of visitors must take them home as souvenirs."

"They're not the valuable ones. Look for privately printed ones or early ones from Kennedy Space Center."

"Here's one showing a big parade for Neil Armstrong on September 6, 1969. It's from his hometown, Wapakoneta, Ohio. Is it a good card?"

"It has potential," Ann said with a soft chuckle. "Watch out, or you'll become a postcard collector yourself."

"Actually, I have thought of framing a few old greeting postcards if I ever happen upon some. Wouldn't they look nice in a grouping? I could change them for different holidays."

"Maybe you should look at your aunt's."

"She may have a new appreciation of them now that she's met you. I'm afraid she'll change her mind about donating them to your hunger auction."

"I never pressure people to give up family mementos," Ann reminded her. "Also I was told that the women's guild at Good Shepherd in Potterston will have a big box for me when I speak at their church tomorrow. I'll have plenty of sorting and organizing to do when I get home."

"It must be time-consuming, putting them in lots."

"That's the fun part. Once the auction appears in the postcard publication, I have to keep track of bids, then notify the high bidders. The hardest part is wrapping all the packages and taking them to the post office. Once I had to do forty for one sale, but that was an unusually large one."

"How many sales have you had?"

"The last one was number forty-four. I've been doing this for nearly twenty years."

Jane was thoughtful for a few minutes.

"I never realized a little thing like a postcard could lead to such a big commitment. Count me in as your Acorn Hill connection. I'm sure there must be people at Grace Chapel who would love to find a good use for cards they've accumulated but don't especially want. I'll bring it up at our church."

When they got to the inn, Ann took all the cards from the old box and asked Jane if she could discard it with the inn's garbage.

"I don't want to take the box inside," she explained. "You never know what's lurking in an old box if it's been in a cellar or attic. A friend accidentally brought a bat home in a box of miscellaneous junk from an auction. They had quite a scare when it flew around inside her house."

"That's something I wouldn't have imagined," Jane said. "I never suspected that there was so much to learn about antiquing."

Louise had just finished cutting the partially frozen round steak into very thin strips for sukiyaki when Jane got home. She'd been glad to prepare the meat so her sister didn't have to hurry home from the tag sale. After her lesson with Diana, she needed jobs to distract her. She wasn't sure that she'd handled the situation at all well. Maybe she should have honored Diana's decision not to drive. It wasn't like her to be insistent with a pupil, and she didn't know how things stood between them now. It would be disappointing to lose Diana as a piano student, but Louise was more certain than ever that the biggest obstacle to passing the road test was not a lack of ability.

Jane was bubbling with enthusiasm over her tag sale experience, and Louise tried to be a good listener. Still, the problem of the last lesson wouldn't go away. Should she cancel? What would that do to Diana's self-confidence? But if she took the road test and failed, she might refuse to try again for years, if at all. The whole Zale family would suffer, at least until the boys were old enough to get licenses. But aside from that, Diana would feel that she'd let her mother and herself down.

"Can you imagine growing up in a house that large?" Jane said. "Think of the games of hide-and-seek. Of course, it's sort of creepy today, all that faded grandeur. The plaster moldings in the ballroom are crumbling away, and I don't know if they can refinish the hardwood floor without ruining the patina."

Louise washed her hands at the kitchen sink and let Jane relate all that she'd seen. She didn't share her sister's enthusiasm for buildings, believing that a house only became a home when there was love present, but Jane's artistic eye had much in common with her own love of music. It enriched her life but didn't overshadow her faith in the Lord and love of those around her.

"I told Aunt Ethel to come at six," Jane said when she'd wound down on her afternoon experiences. "She likes an early dinner, so she'll probably be here before then. The sukiyaki has to be done at the last minute, but I'd better start the steamed rice. Shall we eat in the dining room for a change?"

"Perhaps we should keep to the kitchen," Louise said. "Aunt Ethel enjoys the cozy atmosphere here. She once said it reminds her of fixing dinner for her family when they were all together at the farm."

"You're right. The kitchen it is. Would you mind setting the table? I'm sorry Alice has to work. I wonder if she heard anything about the fawn before she left."

"Yes, I'm delighted to say. Jack and Mark arranged a permanent place at a private animal sanctuary. Last I heard, Jack was going to take it there this afternoon."

"That's wonderful. I hope it works out for the poor creature." Jane started assembling the ingredients. "These are wonderful mushrooms, so firm and white. You're a great shopper, but I feel bad that you went all the way to Potterston for fresh bean sprouts. I could've used canned."

Louise smiled. It was so like Jane to try to make her feel good about herself after the fiasco at breakfast yesterday, but she and Alice had had a good lesson on just how much her talent as a chef contributed to the success of the inn. They were together so much that they sometimes tended to take each other for granted. Louise resolved to correct that tendency.

"You wouldn't have been happy with the results of canned sprouts. What else can I do?"

"Would you rather cut up the celery or slice the water chestnuts?"

"Definitely the celery. I can't possibly do the chestnuts as well as you do."

They worked in quiet companionship as Jane started the rice and dissolved beef bouillon granules in boiling water. Louise knew that if she were a cook, she would never go through all the preparations to make sukiyaki, but Jane was in a happy place all her own when she worked with food. She didn't stop chopping until all the ingredients were lined up ready to go into the big skillet after Ethel got there.

She didn't keep them waiting. "Here I am," she called out as she walked through the front hall and headed toward the kitchen.

"Aunt Ethel, we're in the kitchen," Louise said, walking to the doorway to meet her.

"I brought a pecan pie," their aunt said proudly. "You're always feeding me, so I wanted to bring something special. It's a recipe your mother gave me when I was practically a newlywed."

Louise was touched by the offering. She could also remember her mother making pecan pie, which made Ethel's gift all the more special.

"What are you cooking?" She hovered over the stove where Jane was browning the strips of beef.

"Sukiyaki."

Jane made something of a production in adding ingredients to the skillet, and Louise admired her showmanship. Jane could easily work in a Japanese restaurant where meals were cooked at the table. In fact, Jane could choose to work in almost any kind of food establishment anywhere in the country, which made her loyalty to Grace Chapel Inn all the more endearing.

"My favorite! You really are too good to me," Ethel said.

Jane served the sukiyaki from the stovetop, preferring to keep the remainder warm on a low burner rather than let it cool in a serving dish. After they'd given thanks for their blessings, they began eating.

Meals with their aunt were chatty affairs. She knew more about what happened in Acorn Hill than anyone else the sisters knew, and she was always eager to share the latest happenings. Louise had long ago given up on discouraging her gossip. Fortunately it was never malicious or hurtful. She just enjoyed knowing local business and sharing bits of news.

"How is your driving student doing?" she asked as she daintily forked a bite of the luscious Japanese dish.

"She's doing her best." Louise always thought that what happened between a student and teacher should be confidential. She didn't want any gossip about Diana going outside the family circle. It would be too stressful on her aunt not to repeat anything she heard about her pupil's erratic driving habits.

"I always thought that musical people make good drivers," Ethel said.

"Why would you think that?" Jane asked.

"They have a sense of rhythm. It makes them good at typing too. At least, that's what I've always believed. Would you like me to cut the pie?"

"If you like," Jane said.

As much as she liked visiting, their aunt did run out of steam in the evening. She stayed to help clear the table, then Jane put leftovers in a plastic container for her to take home. When she'd first introduced Ethel to Asian cooking, her aunt had been hesitant about trying it. Now she loved the idea of a delicious meal chock-full of vegetables.

As soon as she could after helping out with the dinner cleanup, Louise went up to her bedroom, planning to go to bed early so she would be well-rested for church in the morning. She did turn out the light earlier than usual, but sleep evaded her. She kept remembering what Ethel had said about musicians being good drivers. Diana had a wonderful sense of rhythm except when she was behind the wheel of a car. A girl who could play the piano as well as she did should be able to master an automobile. Was there a connection between the two skills? Was there any way she could use one talent to improve the other? She'd already compared road signs to musical notes, and Diana had responded well to that suggestion. Could she add to it in a way that would help with the driving test?

Louise wanted to fall asleep, but ideas kept whirling through her mind. Somewhere there was a key to building up Diana's self-confidence and, at the same time, helping her concentrate better on her driving. She went over every teaching technique she'd ever used with her piano students, but the answer eluded her. Only one lesson remained before the road test. Could she possibly make a difference at this late date?

She fell asleep without coming up with an answer.

Chapter Seventeen

*S*unday morning after services, Jack visited briefly with the sisters outside of Grace Chapel to assure them that his trip with Jazzy had gone well and that she was in a wonderful place. The sanctuary was very much to Jack's liking, and he thought that it provided an ideal environment for the deer. Alice hugged him for his kindness, and the sisters returned to the inn delighted by his positive report.

Mark called that evening as Alice was packing cupcakes to take to the hospital the next day. One of the nurses was celebrating her fiftieth birthday, and the staff was going to surprise her with a little party when the morning shift ended. Alice wasn't scheduled to work, but she did want to be there to congratulate her friend.

"Are you working tomorrow?" Mark asked. "I've made arrangements to see the fawn if you can get away."

"Oh, I'd love to." She went on to relate the good news they had received from Jack. "I'm not on the schedule, but I'm going in around three. We're having a surprise birthday party for one of the nurses."

"*Hmm*, I don't know if that would allow enough time."

"Can we do it any other day this week?"

"Afraid not. I'm booked solid. I planned to drive to Acorn Hill early and pick you up, but that would be cutting it close to get you home on time."

"Could I meet you part way?"

"That might work. I've never been anywhere near the sanctuary, but it looks pretty remote. Let me check the exact location."

Alice waited while he consulted his map.

"Actually, it would be great if you could drive to the town of New Corwin. It's about an hour's drive from Potterston. From there it's about fifty, maybe sixty, miles to the sanctuary. Would it be too early to meet at nine o'clock?"

"That sounds perfect. I can go directly to the hospital after we visit the fawn. It's much fairer to you, not having to come all the way to Acorn Hill. You've already done so much to help."

"You know I'm always pleased when I can do something for you."

"I really appreciate it. I won't feel entirely at ease about the fawn until I've seen for myself that she's in a good situation."

Mark laughed softly. "You're the most compassionate person I've ever met."

Alice was a little flustered by his compliment, so she brought up a practical consideration.

"Where should we meet?"

"If the town's as small as it looks on the map, there's probably only one main street. Whoever gets there first should stop at the first convenience store or service station on the way into town. I'll be driving my white SUV."

"Tomorrow at nine then. And thank you once again, Mark."

"Jack O'Hara deserves the credit. He found the place and took the fawn there. I have great respect for that fellow."

"He's been so kind. I'll be sure to pass on your tribute to him."

Monday morning Alice was awake by six and preparing for her trip. Jane was in the kitchen ahead of her, starting preparations for breakfast.

"I'll make whatever you like," she offered as she rolled dough for buttermilk biscuits.

"Oh no, you have your hands full with guests. I'm happy with toast and tea this morning. In fact, I can't wait to get on the road and see what this sanctuary is like."

"I've never heard of the town where you're meeting. No wonder, though. Traveling a bit with Ann made me realize that there are a multitude of tiny places nestled in the hills of Pennsylvania that I haven't visited. I can't imagine living in a more beautiful or interesting state, especially in the spring. I love the fresh, light green of the trees this time of year. I'm always thrilled when I spot a patch of wild flowers or a budding bush. Everything is so alive and vibrant in May."

Alice smiled at her sister's enthusiasm. "I'm going to get an early start since I'm not sure how good the roads are," she said.

"Drive carefully and have a nice trip," Jane said, giving Alice a hug.

Alice knew she was leaving earlier than necessary, but she wanted to get to New Corwin in plenty of time. Mark was a dear to leave work on a Monday to go with her. As head vet, he was constantly tied up in meetings and consultations as well as his hands-on work with the animals at the Philadelphia Zoo. He was as devoted to his charges as she was to the patients who came to the hospital.

As she drove in the countryside, she couldn't help thinking about Louise's experience driving with Diana in unfamiliar territory. The narrow roads that curved and climbed through hilly parts of the state could be intimidating, even to an experienced driver, but Alice loved this part of the country. She'd visited the Midwest with its endless fields of corn, beans and wheat. The Southwest and Big Sky country had an exciting grandeur, but she never felt at home in such places. The cozy hills and valleys where she'd grown up and lived most of her life suited her perfectly.

New Corwin was nestled along a narrow river surrounded by tree-covered vistas. Outside the town, horses and white cattle grazed in hilly pastures where creeks cut across the land in jagged lines. Except for an occasional tractor or truck, the farms seemed unchanged from the time when they were first carved out of the forests. Big weathered barns were built on sturdy stone foundations, and brick houses were flush to the ground in the style of the nineteenth century. A few fields were plowed and newly planted, but much of the land was blanketed in fresh, green vegetation for grazing.

She came to a sign that said New Corwin, but Mark's suggestion that they meet at the first service station or convenience store proved to be a problem. There didn't seem to be a main thoroughfare going into town, at least not on the route she'd taken. She continued past the town looking for a route to the business district and quickly found herself climbing to higher pasture.

"This isn't good," she said aloud, checking her watch to confirm that she was still early.

The few streets she'd passed didn't have any route markers to lead her to the center of town, and she quickly found herself back in the countryside, having bypassed the tiny community. Worse, there didn't seem to be any place nearby to turn around. The road curved, winding its way higher, and she could see no crossroads or driveways to use for reversing her direction. No wonder Louise had been so stressed when Diana was in a similar situation.

The road was just wide enough for two cars going in opposite directions, and she didn't dare risk turning around in the middle. The ditches on either side were deep, and the visibility was poor because of the many curves.

"Where on earth am I going?" she wondered aloud. Surely there would be another town up ahead, but how far was it?

Mark would worry if she was late. It was totally unlike her to miss a meeting time. She accelerated, realizing that she'd been going much slower than necessary as she searched for a turning place.

Poor Diana! This situation was enough to unnerve even an experienced driver. She admired Louise more than ever for not giving up on the lessons. It had to be much harder to sit and watch a young driver make mistakes than it was to have control of the car herself.

At last Alice saw what she needed, a rough track leading into a field. It was only a tractor path, but it offered the best opportunity she'd seen. She turned onto the dirt drive, hoping the mud was dried out enough to keep her from getting stuck. For an anxious moment, it seemed that she would be mired down, but she gunned the engine and managed to back onto the road again.

Her unwanted adventure had taken less than fifteen minutes, but it seemed like an hour. She headed back to New Corwin, hoping for better luck in finding Mark's SUV. No doubt he would be there ahead of her by now.

After turning on the first street going toward the town, she eventually made her way to the two-block business district. There was only one gas station and nothing remotely resembling a convenience store, so she pulled in beside the island of pumps and was greatly relieved to see Mark standing beside his vehicle in a parking area at the far side of the lot. She eased her way into a spot beside him and got out of the car.

"I drove past the town and got stuck on a road with no turnarounds," she explained. "Sorry if I kept you waiting."

"You're right on time. I found a little park where you can leave your car until we get back."

When they got there, they were the only ones in the parking section of a small recreational area with swings and play equipment for children. School was still in session, so they didn't expect much activity around her car while they went to the sanctuary.

Alice began to enjoy the outing once she was riding beside Mark. He had an uncanny sense of direction, which had served him well on his many trips to faraway locations.

The roads weren't well marked in this part of the state, and she was soon confused by the many turns, but Mark drove on with the confidence one might expect from someone traveling in his own town.

"I wonder if Jazzy will really be safe," she said.

"That's what we're going to see," Mark said with an understanding smile.

The first indication that they were near the sanctuary was a big orange sign that warned away hunters.

"Do you think anyone pays attention to NO HUNTING signs?" she asked.

"I'm sure the locals do. They'll know places where it's allowed, and I think most out-of-towners hunt as much as animals do, returning to their favorite grounds year after year. Some even belong to clubs that buy large tracts of land so they'll always have a place to hunt."

Alice shuddered. "All to kill poor animals."

"There are two sides to it," he said. "I have a friend at the University of Wisconsin who's told me some horror stories about the overpopulation of deer. They cause accidents and even deaths on the highways. Sometimes they get into mischief in town. He knew of one that somehow got into a dental office and raised havoc until it crashed through a window to get out. When herds get too large for their territory, they starve, so hunters are needed to keep the population under control in some places."

"I suppose."

Alice knew she could never give her stamp of approval to the activity, but it was probably wrong to condemn hunting. A few years ago a black bear had been spotted near the elementary school playground. She'd been as relieved as the rest of the town when it had been caught and transported to a state park. If the alternative had been to shoot it in order to protect the children, she couldn't have objected.

"There it is," Mark said, slowing for a right turn.

The sign was small, spelling out in neat black letters the name of the sanctuary. Just beyond it, on either side of the roadway, were more NO HUNTING signs.

They followed the unpaved way for a long time; at least it seemed like it to Alice. Mark had slowed to a crawl because the road was rutted and full of potholes.

"This road must discourage visitors as well as hunters," Alice said, knowing her smaller vehicle would bounce all over the place on such rough track.

"That must be their headquarters," he said after making a sharp turn to the left and nodding toward a rustic log building. Although it was built as a traditional cabin, the logs were stripped of bark and weatherproofed. A roof of bright green shingles added to the new appearance, and a pair of outbuildings were modern metal prefabs. Alice looked around, expecting to see holding pens like those at Bellwood Farm, but there was nothing of the sort. She looked a bit anxiously at the bland yellow buildings behind the cabin, hoping Jazzy wasn't going to be confined inside again.

A tall young man with dark-blond hair pulled back in a ponytail and a full golden beard came out to meet them. Although he was casually dressed in worn jeans and a faded plaid shirt, he had an air of authority about him. Alice liked him as soon as he smiled, welcoming them both with an outstretched hand.

"I'm Hal Goodman. Please call me Hal. My wife and I run the place for the foundation. I'm sorry she couldn't be here. She has an appointment in town."

"Hal, this is Alice Howard, and I'm Mark Graves. Thanks to her, the fawn survived after its mother was killed on the highway."

"It's nice to meet you, Hal," said Alice. "I can't tell you how grateful I am that you're taking our fawn."

"And it's nice to meet you both. Mr. O'Hara—quite an impressive animal advocate—spoke highly of you. I just wish we could take every orphan in the state, but we can only introduce so many into the wild every year. Otherwise, our preserve would become so overpopulated that the deer would starve in the winter."

"How did you get started?" she asked.

"A wealthy businessman donated the property to be run as an animal sanctuary. Fortunately he also left a sizable inheritance in trust for the upkeep, and a foundation to oversee it, although we do depend on outside donations too. Our goal is to expand and buy more land as it becomes available. We also release some yearlings onto private property, but only when the site meets our standards for the availability of food and water. Also it has to be remote from humans and posted against hunting."

"Sounds like you have a big responsibility here," Mark said approvingly. "Do you have a vet on call?"

"Yes, sir. We have a retired vet who routinely donates his time. When we run into something serious, we can rely on two others in the area."

"Can we see the fawn?" Alice asked.

"Of course. We can't release her into the wild until she's about four months old, so we have a special fenced area. It's just a short walk."

Alice and Mark followed the lanky young man up the road, turning off onto a footpath that led through large shade trees.

"What a wonderful place for a hike," she said, delighted when they crossed over a small rock-strewn stream spanned by a plank bridge.

"We do allow hikers to use the trails if they get permission first and follow our rules. So far we've been pleased with the way they help us preserve the natural habitat for our wildlife."

The path wound its way down a slight incline with a fenced and gated area at the bottom. It was nothing like the penned area on the farm, and at first Alice didn't see any deer within the confines. It wasn't as densely wooded as the area on either side of the path, but there were more than enough trees and bushes to conceal a sizable number of animals.

"We want them to be shy of humans, although we are still bottle-feeding in this area. It's a dilemma we haven't completely solved, but it helps to have trees and brush where they can conceal themselves. Let's see if we can spot your fawn."

Alice peered into the shadowy areas but was hard-pressed to make out any of the delicate creatures sheltered there. At last she saw movement to her right.

"That's not Jazzy. We call her by the name you gave her, even though we identify the animals by the numbers in our files. When they're young, it's fun to have pet names. There she is." He pointed to the left, and Alice caught a glimpse of a familiar spotted back. Jazzy stepped silently through the underbrush with the grace of a mystical creature.

"I can't imagine a nicer nursery for baby deer," she said, her heart swelling with happiness at the sight of the fawn's perky ears and large, dark eyes.

Jazzy was a wild creature, and it was wonderful that she would live out her life in the best possible habitat. Alice whispered good-bye, dabbed at her misty eyes and caught a grin on Mark's face when he noticed.

As they exited through the gate, Alice turned back for a final glimpse, but the fawn had disappeared into the wooded terrain that was her rightful heritage. Their lives had touched briefly, and Alice felt enriched by the experience.

They walked back, and Hal invited them into his cabin for coffee before they left. It had one big room with a sleeping loft, and the young couple who lived there had made it cozy with colorful braided rugs and quilted throws on the couch and recliner. Their table was fashioned with logs for legs, an inside picnic table with benches instead of chairs. What the cabin lacked in modern conveniences, it more than made up for in warmth. Alice's confidence in the young environmentalist grew as they visited with him.

"We really thank you for taking the fawn," Mark said when they were ready to leave.

"And for showing us her new home. It's a wonderful place," Alice added, putting a brochure that Hal gave her in her shoulder bag as they left.

"Well, what do you think?" Mark asked when they were back in his SUV, slowly bouncing their way out of the sanctuary.

"I can't imagine a better solution. Thank you for making it happen."

She knew that the sanctuary was now on her list of favorite charities.

⌒

Louise couldn't seem to stop humming all day Monday. She had an idea buzzing in her head, and the urge to make music was more than she could resist. Maybe, just maybe, she had a way to boost Diana's confidence before she took her road test.

The big problem was how to approach her pupil without undermining the progress she'd already made. The trip to Potterston had been encouraging. Now she had to convince Diana that she could do just as well with an examiner in the car. Their lesson wasn't scheduled until seven in the evening because it was a school day, which gave her time to work out her strategy.

She arrived at the Zales' home a few minutes early, but Diana was waiting on the front porch.

"Come sit in my car for a minute before we begin. I'd like to talk first."

"Mrs. Smith, there's nothing you can say that will make me less worried about my test."

"Please, get in," Louise said gently.

The girl complied, but her face was a study in misery. "I just want to get it over with."

"I understand, but I have some significant additions to make to our comparisons between music and driving.

Yesterday my aunt said something that started me thinking. She said that musicians are usually good drivers because they have a good sense of rhythm."

"She was wrong."

"It certainly isn't an opinion backed by any kind of research that I know of, but I started thinking of all the vehicles on the road as one huge orchestra. Every driver has his part, and the timing is extremely important. Go too fast, and the piece is ruined. Come in at the wrong time, and everything is thrown off. But the more practice, the smoother the execution."

"I'm not sure I see the connection," Diana said, but the idea had obviously captured her attention.

"The rules of the road are like theory in music. You learn them to improve performance. The tempo is the speed, and the rests are the stops along your way. Eventually you'll learn to sight-read, so strange routes won't throw you. The instrument panel in the car is easier to learn than the keys on a piano, much easier, really. Almost every adult in this country can learn to drive a car, but very few can master a musical instrument as well as you can."

"It's nice of you to say that to build up my confidence," Diana said in a tone that indicated she was hearing but not entirely accepting what Louise was saying.

"Not at all. Confidence will only come when you find it within yourself. Do you know why you did so much better during our last lesson? The road to Potterston is certainly more challenging than the streets of Acorn Hill."

Diana looked at her blankly, not the response Louise had hoped for.

"I think it had everything to do with your being able to focus. What were you thinking about on our last drive?"

"Nothing." Diana shook her head in puzzlement. "Nothing but getting the lesson over with."

"Exactly! Your mind was fully on driving. When you concentrate on just that one thing, you do fine. You wouldn't sit down for a piano recital and think about what happened at school. You would put the whole world out of your mind except for the piece you're playing."

"I think I understand," Diana said hesitantly.

"Wonderful! Come along," Louise said as she got out of her car and led the way to the Zales' vehicle.

She opened the back door and got in behind the driver's seat.

"You're going to sit back there?" Diana asked in surprise.

"No more duets," Louise said firmly. "It's time for you to solo."

"What if I do something wrong?"

"Then you'll find a way to correct it."

"You're my teacher."

"There's absolutely nothing more that I can teach you about an automobile. What you don't know now, you'll have to learn by experience."

"What if we have an accident?"

"The car has airbags, and no doubt some kind of insurance. Are you planning to have an accident?"

"No, I try to be careful."

"Of course you do. No one plans to make mistakes in music or driving. The trick is to practice a lot and keep your mind on what you're doing."

"I really don't think you should ride back there," Diana insisted. "It looks silly, like I'm your chauffeur."

"When you play for a recital, do I sit beside you on the bench?"

"Well, no, but that's different."

"Different in what way? A solo is a solo."

Diana was obviously unhappy, but she got in behind the wheel.

"Now for the prelude. Then you're on your own," Louise said.

"I suppose putting on a seat belt, adjusting mirrors and starting the car is the prelude," Diana said, getting into the spirit of the lesson.

Louise fastened her own seat belt and said a silent prayer that she hadn't put Diana—or herself—in jeopardy.

Diana backed out of the driveway and turned to leave the subdivision, looking carefully and moving cautiously.

"Where should I go?"

"You're the conductor," Louise said.

"I'm going to Potterston. That's where I'll have to take the test."

"Good idea."

Riding in the backseat of the small vehicle, Louise felt every bump in the road. Her knees hit the seat in front of her when Diana made stops, but she couldn't complain about the lack of smoothness in her driving. Diana followed every traffic rule and exercised caution. Her highway driving wasn't bad either. Louise managed to get a peek at the speedometer, and her pupil was driving at exactly the posted speed limit.

"Can we stop for a soda?" Diana asked when they reached Potterston.

"It's entirely your choice."

Diana insisted on treating at a dairy bar, and Louise hadn't enjoyed a root-beer float so much since childhood.

"Is it okay if we drive around town for a while?" Diana asked.

"Take as long as you like."

Louise didn't bring up homework or the time her mother expected her back. This was Diana's solo. It was her decision when to end the driving session.

"Will you please sit in front?" Diana asked. "It feels so odd having you behind me."

"I'll be happy to."

The lesson ran considerably overtime, and the sun was setting by the time they started back toward Acorn Hill. Dusk was a difficult time to drive, but Louise didn't give any cautionary instructions. She was tempted to mention their experience with the fawn, but when Diana saw a DEER CROSSING sign, she slowed appropriately to keep an eye on the shadowy areas along the road.

The last light of day was fading away when they reached the Zales' home. Diana parked in the garage, something she wouldn't have tried a week earlier, but she didn't get out of the car.

"I am so grateful to you for helping me," she said. "Whether I pass my test tomorrow or not, you've been the best driving teacher I've had."

"You're going to pass. You have the rhythm of driving now, and you realize how important it is to concentrate."

As she drove home to the inn, Louise hoped that she was right. It was all up to Diana now.

Chapter Eighteen

ane was in a happy mood Tuesday morning. The breakfast guests had raved over her homemade corned beef hash and eggs, made from a recipe in the book she'd bought while antiquing with Ann. They'd all been lovely people, a nice contrast to certain other guests who had recently visited the inn.

Her sisters had also been especially cheerful at the family breakfast that followed the guests' meal. Alice's mind was greatly relieved after her visit to the animal sanctuary, and they'd tossed around ideas for contributing to the worthwhile work done there. Louise's last driving lesson with Diana had gone better than any that had preceded it. She wasn't sure whether her pupil would pass the road test, but at least she had the satisfaction of knowing she'd done all she could.

Since this was Ann's last evening at the inn, Jane had put together a small dinner party to say good-bye and thank her for the lovely excursions they'd shared. Ethel was coming, and Viola had agreed to join them too. She'd asked

Jack and Alison O'Hara, but they regretfully declined because they were involved in activities with their sons. Jane was sorry that Mark was too busy with his work and too far away to invite. It would have been nice to thank all the people who'd helped them in the past couple of weeks.

It was a treat for Jane to prepare a special dinner. She had it all planned, including Rock Cornish hens served individually to each guest. The meal would be elegant but not overly time-consuming to prepare.

With her plans made and her kitchen chores under control, Jane was ready to treat herself to some time in the garden. She donned her big straw hat and went out to see what needed doing most urgently. To her delight, the spring flowers were in full bloom, including tulips in an assortment of bright colors lining the garden path. The nicest thing about Grace Chapel Inn's garden was that it was delightfully different every season.

Jane went to the gardening shed, now cleared of all traces of the fawn's stay, and got her gloves and the tools she needed. She was walking to a bed that needed spading when something on the ground caught her eye. Her first thought was that Wendell had dragged home something unpleasant and dead, but she saw a flicker of movement. The tiny, pinkish blob was a baby bird and, against all odds, it seemed to be alive.

Jane looked around for the nest, but apparently it was too high or too well hidden to be visible. Returning the baby bird to its nest didn't seem to be an option, but neither did leaving it on the ground. Much as she adored Wendell, she had to recognize that even the casual curiosity of a cat would be fatal to the helpless bird.

Bending beside it, she very carefully scooped it up in her gloved hand, a little nervous because the creature was so frail. It barely weighed anything in her palm, and she didn't have a clue what to do with it. At least it didn't seem to be injured, if the little flickering movements were an indication. She needed a place to put it. Moving with care, she carried it into the house and found one of the plastic containers that she used to put leftovers in the freezer. The poor little thing looked so helpless and forlorn that she wondered whether she was doing a kindness by bringing it inside.

What on earth should she do next?

Alice would know. "Alice, where are you?" Jane yelled, amused at herself because it had been a long time since she'd cried out so loudly for her big sister.

"What's wrong?" Alice hurried toward her from the parlor, where she'd been dusting.

"Look what I found."

"Oh my." Alice peered into the plastic container. "Were you planning to freeze it?"

Jane smiled at her sister's humor. "I don't have a clue what to do with it. Orphans are your specialty."

"You didn't see the nest, did you?"

"No. It could be up in the eaves, I suppose, but the mother has it well hidden."

"Well, we'll just have to see what we can do about it."

"I think that's going to be *you*, not *we*."

Alice smiled. Jane knew that this was a foundling that her sister could feel confident about helping. She fully expected it to be able to fly away some day.

"It will need water and food soon, I imagine," Alice said, already making plans. "Digging worms isn't my favorite activity, but this is an emergency."

"I can help you there," Jane offered.

"No, you have too much else to do. I'll take care of it. I wonder what kind of bird it is. We'll just have to see when it gets feathers. I wonder if I can find that book Father consulted to identify species. First, I have to find a better place to keep it. And it has to have a name. Let me think."

She stared hard at the tiny creature, and Jane didn't interrupt her thoughts.

"In the Book of Luke, Jesus said that God knew every sparrow even though five were sold for two pennies. I think I'll call him Luke. It's a grand name for such a tiny bird. Tiny or not, he's one of God's creatures. Yes, I'll call him Luke."

Jane grinned. "Or *her*."

Alice didn't hear. She was already carrying her new charge to the pantry in search of a temporary resting place for it.

Jane stood for a moment, lost in thought. How wonderful that God had provided her with two amazing sisters. Alice's pleasure in the bird was one more reminder of what a caring and loving person she was.

Thank you, Lord, for having so richly blessed my life, especially in the love my sisters share with me.

Louise finished her last piano lesson of the day and wandered into the kitchen in case Jane needed help, but her mind was on Diana. This was her student's big day, and she couldn't help thinking about the road test. If Diana did as well as she had in her last lesson, there was a good chance she would pass. Unfortunately, she was her own worst enemy. If she allowed the testing procedure to interfere with her concentration, all the lessons in the world wouldn't help.

"What can I do for you?" she asked her sister.

"Would you mind setting the table in the dining room? There will be six of us. Use the good china. I've already put on the tablecloth. It was a job getting the stains out after the Brown girl smeared egg and who knows what else on it.

I'm torn between feeling sorry for her and wanting to teach her some manners."

"We won't be seeing them again," Louise said mildly. "Something smells wonderful."

"Ann's farewell dinner. I'll be sad to see her leave. She's been a marvelous guest."

"Maybe she'll come back another time."

"I hope so. The inn seems so much more lively when it brings us such special people."

"Is anyone here?" someone called from the main entrance.

Louise recognized her aunt's voice and went to greet her in the front hall. Ethel was carrying a brown paper grocery bag, which she slipped behind the reception desk in a furtive way. Louise was curious, but she wouldn't spoil her aunt's little game by asking what it was.

"Jane is finishing dinner. You can help me set the table if you like, Aunt Ethel."

"Oh, please go on without me. I want to have a word with Jane," she said mysteriously.

Louise smiled as she went about setting the places for dinner. The dining room had an old-world charm with its elegant mahogany table and buffet, and it was a treat to entertain friends there.

She was just putting on the final touches when there was a rather frenzied knocking at the front door. Since guests came and went as they wished, the door was never locked during the day. Viola would probably just walk in when she arrived for dinner. Louise hurried to see who was making such a commotion.

When Louise opened the door, Diana was about to knock again. Her hair was spilling wildly around her flushed face, and she seemed too out of breath to talk. Louise's heart went out to her, sure that her agitation meant she'd failed her test. She was trying to think of a way to comfort her when Diana flew into her arms and gave her a big hug.

"I passed, Mrs. Smith! I passed! I owe it all to you." She stepped back with a huge grin on her face.

"Wonderful! I'm so pleased, Diana, but it's your doing, not mine."

"I drove here by myself, my first real solo. I couldn't wait to tell you. The only problem I had with the test was parallel parking. It took me three tries to do it right, but the inspector said that wasn't bad. A lot of people have trouble with it."

"Congratulations, Diana. I couldn't be more pleased."

"I can't stay. Dad is out of town, so I'm driving Mom and the boys to a restaurant for dinner to celebrate. I just wanted to thank the person who made it possible."

"That's you," Louise said with a broad smile.

As she watched Diana leave, Louise was thankful that she hadn't given up on the girl. Diana's happiness at passing the road test was worth all the strain of the lessons.

Jane listened to her aunt's idea and was putting the finishing touches on her dinner when Ann came downstairs in another of her elegant costumes, this time crimson taffeta overlaid with chiffon in shades of gold, orange and red. She seemed to use the same pattern for all her outfits, but the effect was always rather spectacular. Jane felt plain indeed in beige slacks and a simple mocha-brown knit top, but then, few women could present themselves with Ann's flair. She turned her height and statuesque build into an asset by dressing dramatically.

"I'm going to miss this lovely place," Ann said to Jane in the kitchen. "My vacation has been wonderful. I've already talked to my friend who couldn't come, and we're going to try again next summer. I can't think of a better place for a vacation than Grace Chapel Inn, or better hosts than the Howard sisters."

"I hate to see you leave," Jane admitted. "I had a wonderful time on our excursions."

"You made them a lot more fun for me."

"Where is everyone?" Viola called out.

"In here." Jane took one last peek at the golden-brown hens in the oven and stood to greet her. "Aunt Ethel and Louise are finishing up in the dining room. Alice is out checking on her baby bird one more time before dinner. This is our guest, Ann Baldwin. Ann, this is Viola Reed. She owns Nine Lives Bookstore. It was our good luck that she was driving on the highway when Alice and Louise found the fawn."

"We met when Ann came to the store," Viola said. "I was thrilled to meet someone who loves *Anna Karenina* as much as I do."

"Hope I haven't held up dinner," Alice said, coming in from the side door. "I just wanted to check on Luke. He's in the shed."

"Her bird," Jane explained. "He fell from his nest." They all found their seats at the dining-room table, and Alice asked a special blessing on the friends who were sharing their meal.

"Loving Father," she began, "we ask Your blessing on those assembled here. Our words will never be adequate to express our boundless gratitude for the friendship and love in our lives and for Your manifold blessings."

When she finished, she asked the others if they would like to add any thanks of their own.

"Thanks be to God for the opportunity to serve others, and especially for the new confidence Diana has found," Louise said.

"And thank You, Lord, for the bounty all around us and for friends new and old," Jane added.

"I am so thankful for loving nieces who welcome me into their home and lives," Ethel said.

"I'm thankful for the opportunity to know the Howard sisters and to share briefly in the love they bring to everyone's life," Ann said.

"And for all God's creatures. Amen," Viola concluded.

Alice offered to help Jane serve, but she insisted that everyone stay seated.

They began with baby-spinach salads and homemade poppy seed rolls. She dished up the main course in the kitchen, delivering each golden-brown Rock Cornish hen on a bed of wild rice and almonds. Steaming carrots and string beans waited in separate dishes.

"I'm speechless," Ann said after she cut through the crackly brown skin and tasted the succulent poultry. "There simply are no words for how delicious this is."

"Before I forget," Viola said, "I have good news. I'm awaiting my first-ever litter of Siamese kittens. I already have people on a waiting list to take one of them."

"That's wonderful," Alice said. "Of course, you know we are not in a position—"

"Oh, I'm not here to recommend another Howard adoption," Viola said chuckling.

Conversation flowed with the ease found only with people who genuinely like each other, but Jane couldn't help noticing that their aunt was unusually quiet.

"Aunt Ethel has been very helpful to us," she said, wanting to draw her into the conversation. "She was the one who suggested we feed the fawn with a rubber glove."

"Yes," Louise said, "and she reminded me that musicians make good drivers just when I was ready to give up on Diana. I'm so happy that she passed her road test today. Thank you for your input, Aunt Ethel."

"I try to help out." It was a subdued response that wasn't characteristic of their aunt.

"Are you all right?" Jane asked, worried that the older woman was concealing some problem.

"Oh my, yes. I'm fine. I just have something on my mind. You know those postcards I showed you?"

"Of course," Ann said, "and it's perfectly all right if you want to preserve them as part of your family heritage."

"That's just it. I want them to go to your hunger project, but I don't want my nieces to think I'm giving away Bob's family history. Jane told me before dinner that she doesn't want any of the cards, but I want to be sure I'm not making a mistake."

"If your children don't want them, you couldn't possibly put them to a better use," Jane assured her. "I'm sure you'll always remember your husband in your heart. The postcards are only objects." Louise and Alice nodded in agreement.

"Most aren't even connected to people I knew," Ethel admitted.

She got up abruptly and left the table. Jane used the opportunity to clear away the dinner plates and bring out dessert, pineapple upside-down cake. It was made using an old family recipe and had been one of their father's favorite desserts. By the time she topped it with whipped cream and gave everyone a serving, Ethel had returned to the table with her brown paper bag.

"I put them all in plastic bags. That box was too old and battered to use for such lovely cards. I sorted them by types," she said, taking some out to show the group. "Here are all the Christmas and Easter greetings. And look at these cards. It's hard to realize how much things have changed. Some still have horses and buggies in the pictures."

"This is so sweet of you, Ethel," Ann said. "They'll be in the next sale, and I'm sure they'll add up to a very nice donation to fight hunger."

Ethel glowed as everyone at the table praised her generosity. After they finished dessert, she was the one who suggested they go to the parlor where, perhaps, Louise could be persuaded to play for them.

They gathered around the piano, and Jane was surprised to find her eyes moist. It was joy, not sadness, that made tears well up. With faith, love and friendship in her life, she counted herself among the most blessed of women.

About the Authors

*P*am Hanson and Barbara Andrews are a daughter-mother writing team. They began working together in the early 1990s and have had twenty books published, including fifteen under the pseudonym Jennifer Drew.

Pam has taught reporting courses at West Virginia University and is now director of advising for the School of Journalism. She has presented writing workshops and has been involved in school and church activities. She lives with her husband, a professor, and their two sons in West Virginia, where she shares her home with her mother.

Previous to their partnership, Barbara had twenty-one novels published under her own name. She began her career writing Sunday-school stories and contributing to antiques publications. Currently she writes a column and articles about collectible postcards. For twenty years she has sponsored a mail postcard auction with all proceeds going to world hunger relief. She is the mother of four and the grandmother of seven.

Tales from Grace Chapel Inn

Back Home Again
by Melody Carlson

The Start of Something Big
by Sunni Jeffers

Recipes & Wooden Spoons
by Judy Baer

Spring Is in the Air
by Jane Orcutt

Hidden History
by Melody Carlson

Home for the Holidays
by Rebecca Kelly

Ready to Wed
by Melody Carlson

Eyes on the Prize
by Sunni Jeffers

The Price of Fame
by Carolyne Aarsen

Summer Breezes
by Jane Orcutt

We Have This Moment
by Diann Hunt

Tempest in a Teapot
by Judy Baer

The Way We Were
by Judy Baer

Mystery at the Inn
by Carolyne Aarsen

The Spirit of the Season
by Dana Corbit

Saints Among Us
by Anne Marie Rodgers

Keeping the Faith
by Pam Hanson & Barbara Andrews

Once you visit the charming village of Acorn Hill, you'll never want to leave. Here, the three Howard sisters reunite after their father's death and turn the family home into a bed-and-breakfast. They rekindle old memories, rediscover the bonds of sisterhood, revel in the blessings of friendship and meet many fascinating guests along the way.